Living the Dream
Life's Outtakes - Year 16

52 Humorous and Inspirational Short Stories

By
Daris Howard

A collection of stories, humorous anecdotes, thoughts, and tidbits of wisdom from the newspaper column *Life's Outtakes*.

Publishing Inspiration

Living Dream

Life's Outtakes - Year 16

52 Humorous and Inspirational Short Stories

By

Daris W. Howard

A collection of stories, humorous anecdotes, thoughts, and tidbits of wisdom from the newspaper column *Life's Outtakes*.

ISBN-10: 1-62986-027-1
ISBN-13: 978-1-62986-027-5

www.publishinginspiration.com

Publishing Date: May 4, 2023

Publishing Inspiration LLC

Table of Contents

Dear Reader,

People often ask me if my stories are true. Though I admit that I tend to take a bit of literary license in my writing, each story is based on an actual event. Sometimes the stranger stories are the ones that are stretched the least. As people often say, truth is stranger than fiction.

I also want to note that some of the names have been changed to protect the anonymity of the individuals.

Daris Howard

A Reason Why

By all accounts from the hospital staff, Bart had died. He had been in a wreck, and when the emergency crew arrived on the scene, he barely had a pulse. Bart was life-flighted to the nearest regional hospital, and the nurses and doctors did everything they could to save him.

Bart was well-loved in our community, and word spread quickly. Many people started fasting and praying. But despite it all, eventually, the hospital said they had lost him. But then something happened, and he came back. Bart didn't really want to come back, and he was not at all pleased at being here.

"I'm not afraid of dying," he said. "It's the process of getting there that I don't relish, and I didn't want to have to do it twice."

To add to his displeasure, he found that many of his internal organs didn't work as well as they previously had. Some things had to be removed to save his life, and what was left worked at a subpar level. He said that if the fasting and praying had brought him back, he was not the slightest bit pleased with it.

Bart often asked why he had to come back. One day at church, he specifically cornered me to ask that question.

"Bart, I can't tell you why some things happen," I replied. "But I feel everything has a reason. Sometime something will happen, and you will feel that your question will at least partly be answered. However, you may never know the full reason until your life is ending."

Bart tried to deal with his changed life the best he could. He worked through his health issues and learned to live with the ones he could not change. He struggled to do everything he could before and had to adjust to letting his sons do more of the farm work. It was a big adjustment, and he tried not to complain, but he still struggled with the question of why. And with that question came the personal doubts about himself and the value of his life.

But all of that changed one day. On that day, a group of Bart's grandsons, along with a few friends, decided to work on some old four-wheelers and snow machines in Bart's shop. The machines hadn't run in years, and the boys were trying to get them started. They were using extra gasoline to try to get the engines to fire when something went terribly wrong.

A spark from one machine lit the gasoline on fire, and that caught the gas can on fire. A huge flame shot out and engulfed the portion of the room closest to the door. They tried to get the door open, but with the fire burning too hot near it, the heat drove them back. The fire shot up to the ceiling, and once it had burned a hole through the sheetrock, it raced with the flame of an air-fired forge through the rafters.

Unable to help with the equipment his sons were working on, a discouraged Bart had decided to go home. That was when he saw the smoke. He rushed to his shop and quickly realized there had to be someone inside. He braved the heat and smoke to get the door open and quelled the fire there enough so he could get all the boys out.

The boys were taken to the hospital, and though they all had smoke inhalation and burns, the doctor said they would all recover. But then he said something to Bart that made him rethink his question on the value of his life. The doctor said, "If you had not been there, arriving when you did, none of the boys would be alive."

Bart considered that maybe there truly was an important reason for his life after all, and he was glad he came back despite the challenges.

Rooster Pox

Alice loved the chickens. It was her job to gather the eggs each day, and though the family didn't have names for the chickens, she secretly did and knew each one. She became familiar with the most common nesting places and was good at finding the eggs around the yard. Yes, she loved the chickens.

But the rooster was another matter. Alice hated the rooster. He didn't pick on anyone else in the family—only her. Maybe it was because she was youngest, and since she was only five years old, he was about the same height as she was. And when he stood up on his claws and bristled his wings, she felt he was even taller.

He had chased after Alice more than once, causing her to throw down her basket of eggs and run for her life. She hadn't broken a lot of eggs that way, but there had been a few. When she complained to her dad about it, he lovingly took her on his lap.

"Alice," he said, "you've got to let the rooster know you aren't afraid of him."

"But I am afraid of him," Alice replied.

"Well, act like you're not. Act like you are going to knock his cluck into the middle of next week, and he will learn to respect you."

Alice tried to stand up to the rooster, but the minute he bristled the feathers on his head, she ran. He just seemed to get ornerier and ornerier. But one day it all came to a head.

Her dad had brought home a watermelon from the market, and Alice ate a good helping. Pretty soon, she needed to visit the outhouse. But as she started toward it, she stopped dead in her tracks. Standing in front of it was the rooster. He turned to face Alice as if daring her to come any closer.

Alice retreated, but it wasn't long before matters were getting quite desperate. She hid where she could monitor the outhouse door but not be seen. Finally, the rooster went around the back, and Alice dashed from her hiding place. She made it safely to the outhouse, ran inside, and slammed the board down that locked the door shut.

Alice did her business, and feeling much relieved, lifted the latch and opened the door. To her dismay, there stood the rooster. There was a short stare-down before Alice slammed the door and locked it. Alice kept looking out the door for over an hour, only to find the rooster was still standing guard.

It was summer, and the smell and the heat started to get to her. Alice began calling for help, and did for a long time, until she was almost hoarse. Everyone else was busy doing their own work. Finally, the family realized Alice was missing and searched for her. However, no one thought to look in the outhouse. At least, no one did until someone needed to use it. At that point, the rooster was relieved of guard duty, and Alice was freed.

The next day, Alice started to get red spots all over her. They itched horribly. She thought she was going to scratch herself to death.

"You'll be okay," her mother told her. "You just have a bad case of chickenpox."

"I knew it," Alice said. "I knew it was from the rooster keeping me shut up in the outhouse."

"Chickenpox doesn't come from chickens," her father replied.

But nothing anyone said could convince her that her sickness was from anything other than the rooster. No one else got them. Of course, everyone else had already had the disease, but trying to explain that to Alice didn't help. Her mind was made up. And her older brothers' teasing didn't help. They kept saying Alice had "rooster pox."

Her dad finally gave in. "Maybe it's time for the rooster to go."

Once she was well, Alice returned to her chore of gathering eggs. But even with the rooster gone, it took a long time for the timidity she felt gathering eggs to go away. She kept vigilant, always looking over her shoulder.

And it took children of her own getting chickenpox before Alice finally believed chickenpox didn't come from chickens—or at least roosters.

A Need to Listen

I started a new job at a potato warehouse. Learning that I had grown up on a farm, the owner immediately assigned me to drive potato trucks from the potato cellars to the warehouse and back. It wasn't a bad job. At least I wasn't working on the potato sorting lines.

Typically, two cellars were working simultaneously to keep up with the volume of potatoes that were needed at the warehouse. I would drive a truck from one of them to the warehouse, where they would have an empty truck waiting for me. I would then be told which cellar needed the empty truck. My job was to make sure there were always potatoes flowing into the warehouse and that no cellar was ever waiting for a truck.

The crew in the cellars, with me driving, worked efficiently to make sure everything kept running. Because there was only one to drive for both cellars, sometimes loads backed up. That would mean I had to work through lunch, trying to grab a little food while I drove.

One night, after an exceptionally long day, I had just arrived home when I received a call. It was the warehouse foreman.

"Daris," he said, "we have enough people sick that we will be down to one crew in the potato cellars. That means it will really push you guys to keep the warehouse supplied with potatoes. I'm checking to see if the cellar crew can start at six in the morning so we can have all the trucks full when we start. That way, you'll hopefully be able to keep us rolling."

I told him I would be there at six. He then hung up to call

others on our crew.

The following day, by six, I was moving all the trucks to the operating cellar. A young man named Steven gave me rides back and forth to the other cellar so I could move the trucks from there. Soon all the trucks were at the working cellar, and I started driving the full ones to the warehouse. Once more, Steven shuttled me back to the cellar each time to get the next truck.

By eight o'clock, when the warehouse started, all the trucks except for two were full and lined up at the warehouse, ready to be unloaded. Steven took me back to the cellar, and from that point, my job was supposed to run the same as usual.

When I drove the next load to the warehouse, I parked it in the line to be unloaded. There were no trucks yet empty, so I took a breather and sat down on a bench outside of the warehouse. I felt it was a well-deserved break, especially since I often had to work so many of my lunch hours.

However, the warehouse owner was a demanding boss. The last thing he wanted to see was someone idle. I hadn't seen him come out the door, but his attention was immediately drawn to me sitting there.

"What do you think you're doing sitting around?" he demanded.

I stood and turned to him. "I'm waiting for. . ."

He never even let me finish. "I can see you're waiting! And that means the warehouse will be waiting for potatoes. Get your tail in gear and get a truck and get back to the cellar."

"But there are no trucks that are. . . "

I was trying to tell him there were no empty trucks, but again he cut me off again. "What do you mean there are no trucks? Of course, there are trucks." He then pointed at one. "Grab that one and get it back to the cellar."

"But it's. . ."

"I don't want any excuses," he said. "Get it and get it back to the cellar now!"

I shrugged and went to the truck. He watched me until I drove away. I was just about back to the cellar when Steven came roaring up in the pickup.

"The warehouse foreman wants to know what you're thinking about taking a full truck back to the cellar."

"What I'm thinking," I replied, "is that I wish some people would listen to their workers who know what is going on."

When I got the truck back to the warehouse and explained what had happened to the foreman, he rolled his eyes. "It's not the first time something like that has happened. Someday someone needs to tell the owner some things."

It's probably good I didn't tell him what I really thought when he told me to take the full truck to the cellar.

Hating Goats

Lilly had a terrible dislike of goats, and she didn't know why. It seemed a little beyond reason. She couldn't find the slightest enjoyment, even in the little ones. While other children would play with the goats and pet them, she would walk away in disgust.

When she became a teenager, the neighbors got some baby goats. Many people in their rural community gathered to pet them and feed them handfuls of grass and hay. But Lilly didn't even want to go see them. She only went with the others under duress from her friends' teasing, and she stood away from the pen, rolling her eyes in disgust.

"Don't you at least think they're cute?" her younger sister asked.

"Not a bit," Lilly replied.

"You know, Lilly," her mother said, "you really ought to work on your attitude about goats. Goats can be quite useful."

"In what way?" Lilly asked.

"They can eat down weeds," Lilly's mother replied.

"And some people milk them," Lilly's sister said.

"And if they're big and ornery, they can smash things," Lilly's older brother said. "Especially if they are males and have big horns."

The way he said it made Lilly think there was more to his statement than the words indicated. Their mother must have thought so, too.

"Matthew, is there something more you want to tell us?" their mother asked.

"Like what?" Matthew asked innocently.

"There seems to be something behind your words that you're holding back."

"Really?" Matthew replied.

"Really," their mother replied. "Why don't you share it with us?"

Matthew looked at the others staring at him and slowly said, "Well, there might have been a minor incident some years ago."

"Go on," their mother said.

Then the story came out.

Some years earlier, when Lilly was about three, some of Ethan's friends had a mean billy goat with big horns. The boys would jump the fence and get the goat to chase them. They would scramble to safety over the fence poles at the last minute and watch the goat slam full force into the wood. The goat would then shake his head and bleat out a warning to any would-be trespassers. The boys loved it and would laugh and do it again.

But one day, one boy was too slow, and the goat caught him with his horns. The boy got a broken leg out of the deal, and none of them dared climb in the pen with the goat again.

Not wanting to lose their fun, they tried to figure out what else they could do. They would twirl sticks through the fence, throw an end of a rope over, or wave clothes at the goat. But the goat didn't charge. That was what they were doing when little three-year-old Lilly came wandering by. One of the neighbor boys instantly had an idea. The boys, with their adolescent mentality, never considered the possible consequences of their actions. Instead, they held Lilly over the fence, and the goat charged. They pulled her out well before the goat hit the fence.

Her screams not only brought the goat charging at them, but it brought their mother from the house. The boys realized that it had been a stupid idea. Ethan admitted he trembled at the thought of what might have happened, and that he could have hurt his little sister. All the boys were glad Lilly was safe, and nothing really bad had happened during their lack of judgment. And they never bothered the goat again.

The boys pretended innocence and never admitted to it. Ethan said Lilly never seemed to like goats after that.

"Oh, and I wonder why?" Lilly said sarcastically. "And to be honest, I'm beginning to wonder how I feel about certain boys, too."

But knowing a possible reason why she felt as she did helped Lilly. After that, she even began to like goats a little—at least, the baby ones.

Teaching and Learning

✦

Samantha had just finished college with a teaching degree in elementary education. She was excited to get out and work with children. But first, she had to decide where she wanted to go.

Having grown up in a big city, and seldom having been outside of it, she decided she wanted to go somewhere rural. Her college advisor visited with her about that decision.

"You know, Samantha, maybe you should reconsider that decision," he said. "Going where the culture differs from what you are used to might not be a good idea. You might want to get some teaching experience under your belt first."

"I'm not leaving the U.S.," Samantha replied. "I just plan to get out of the city."

"I understand that," her advisor said. "But even in the same country, another region can be a culture shock when there are things a person is not used to. For example, I grew up in a wealthy school district that had funds to hire music teachers. I sang in choirs and played in the band. So, when I graduated and went to work for a small rural school, I was assigned to teach choir one hour each day. Most of those kids had never even seen a choir before and couldn't carry a tune in a bucket."

Samantha laughed. "I think I'll be okay."

Samantha was well qualified and was readily hired by a small school in rural Idaho. She worked up the best lesson plans and acquired all the finest materials. Class went okay until the second week when she had her first show-and-tell day. She had never imagined anyone bringing a goat to school.

Samantha had to admit that Johnny's pygmy goat was cute. Samantha probably should have made Johnny hold it in his arms while he talked. But she definitely shouldn't have let him put it on her desk so everyone could "see it better."

As Johnny was telling about his goat, it started munching on Samantha's lesson plan. When Samantha saw the final remains of her well-laid-out outline sliding into the goat's mouth, she did something else she shouldn't have done—she screamed. The sudden loud noise scared the goat so badly it wet all over Samantha's desk.

The rest of the morning was pretty much useless, at least as far as teaching. The class materials were ruined, and it took almost the entire morning to clean up the mess. Added to that was the fact that she was so flustered she couldn't think straight enough to teach anything for the rest of the day.

Samantha decided she would ban animals for show-and-tell. But when she did, some of the children got very upset. She began to understand that animals were an integral part of her children's lives. Growing up in an apartment in the city, she hadn't had any pets. The apartment building didn't allow them. So, she decided she needed to let them bring the animals, but she vowed she would be more on guard.

But being on guard didn't prepare her for the morning that Kevin rode his horse to school. The last bell was just ringing when Kevin led the horse into the classroom. Samantha was writing on the board with her back to the class. When she turned around, the horse stuck its nose in her face and snorted.

Samantha jumped backward, slamming into the chalkboard as the children laughed. While she tried to wipe the snot from her face and hair, Kevin told all about raising the horse from a little filly to a full-grown mare. Samantha determined she would look up the word 'filly' to see what it meant.

After Kevin led his horse from the room, Samantha tried to regain her composure. That worked until Mr. Johnson, the janitor, who also drove the bus and mowed the lawns, stopped by the classroom. He didn't appreciate Kevin's horse chewing and fertilizing his nicely cut grass.

That was when Samantha decided she must do something else. She didn't want to stop the kids from bringing their pets. But what could she do? She came up with the perfect idea.

She would have a pet day.

(Continued)

Teaching and Learning

(Part 2)

Samantha had wanted to teach in a rural school district after having grown up in a big city. However, she wasn't prepared for everything there. After having a disaster with a goat and a horse for show and tell, she decided something had to be done. She realized the children were attached to their animals, but they couldn't continue bringing them and disrupting the class. She hit on the perfect idea—pet day, held outside on the school lawn.

There was only one teacher per grade in the grade school, and she asked the others if they wanted to join in. All did, but a few of the older, more experienced ones seemed a bit reluctant. Though they gave no specifics, they shared their misgivings about such an event.

The parents were invited to bring the pets and stay for the hour that was scheduled for it. Samantha didn't want the children to bring the animals and then have the pets stuck at the school all day.

There were all kinds of animals. Kevin had his horse, and Johnny brought his goat. Jason brought one of his little piglets. Susan brought a beautiful golden retriever. Ellen brought her Siamese cat. And there were many more. The children moved around and visited with the others about each other's pets. The parents stood on the side and visited with each other, ever ready to lend a hand. Everyone was involved, and Samantha thought it was one of the best ideas she had ever had.

Samantha also moved around, visiting with each child about their pets and asking them questions to help them feel important. When Samantha got to Tanya, she was surprised to see her holding a skunk in her arms.

"Wow," Samantha said. "I've never seen a skunk in real life. I've only seen pictures of them in books. What's her name?"

Tanya beamed. "Flower, like in Bambi. But she's a girl."

"How long have you had her?" Samantha asked.

"Since she was a baby," Tanya replied.

"Was it hard to get her descented?" Samantha asked.

"De what?" Tanya said with a puzzled look.

"Descented," Samantha repeated.

"What does that mean?" Tanya asked.

Samantha smiled. She realized she was using a fifty-dollar word when she should use something more of a dollar value. "It means making it so your skunk can't spray."

Just then, Susan's retriever caught sight of Ellen's cat. The retriever broke free of Susan's grasp, and a chase ensued, around, under, and amid all the animals. Many of the animals tried to make a getaway, but the parents quickly jumped in to help restrain them. The cat was fast and had soon climbed a tree to safety. Samantha breathed a sigh of relief.

Susan's father was just about to grab the retriever's leash when it saw what must have appeared to it as another cat in Tanya's arms.

The retriever came toward Tanya and her skunk at full speed, barking as it came. The skunk, with an inborn sense of defense, flipped around in Tanya's arms and pointed its cannon end toward the oncoming dog. Unfortunately for Samantha, that was also the side she was on. Just as the dog came in range, the skunk sent out a shotgun blast.

16

Samantha fell to the ground coughing, the retriever let out a yelp, and animals scattered everywhere. Even the parents couldn't restrain most of them. Samantha couldn't see or breathe as the ensuing tumult occurred. The skunk saw an open door of the school and sought safety inside, where it continued to air its grievances.

The school was closed for a few weeks, and Samantha had to be gone even longer. The children thought it was a fun break, though the parents were of a different opinion.

After multiple, useless baths in everything from vinegar to tomato juice, Samantha considered that maybe the pet day was not such a great idea after all.

(Continued)

Teaching and Learning

(Part 3)

Growing up in a big city and coming to teach in a small school in rural Idaho, Samantha had a lot to learn. When her idea for a pet day turned into chaos after Tanya brought a skunk, Samantha was sure she would be fired. The school was closed for two weeks to air it out, and Samantha had to stay away for even longer because she had been right by the firing end of the skunk. But when she came back, to her surprise, no one seemed angry.

When she timidly brought it up, the principal just laughed. "Oh, those things happen now and then."

"Not where I came from," Samantha thought. The thought of a skunk at a city school just made her cringe.

She got a little teasing since the smell still lingered, but no one was mean. Most people just laughed when they talked about it. "My daddy said it was something interesting to write in his journal," Johnny said.

If Samantha said that everything was normal after that, she'd be lying—at least not the normal she was used to. There was the day the children couldn't go out to recess because a moose decided he owned the playground. A Fish and Game office was called to drive it off.

Then there was the day she was late to school because someone was driving a herd of sheep down the road. She followed for quite a while until the old shepherd said, "Lady, just ease up to them, and they will gradually move." She did, and the great white woolly sea slowly parted, and she gradually drove through, out of Egypt, to the promised land of open highway.

Whenever she thought she had surely seen everything, something new happened. She had just had that very thought the day she had the episode with Timmy.

Other teachers had warned her that Timmy and all his brothers were slightly autistic. They also all had an insatiable curiosity. Timmy would come to school in clean clothes every day, but by the end, he was always covered head to toe in dirt, or leaves, or who knows what. At first, this flustered Samantha, but gradually she realized it was part of who he was.

Samantha did not know Timmy had taken a curious interest in a female crab spider at recess that day. It was big and ready to lay its eggs. Timmy lay on his stomach watching it the whole recess period. When the bell rang, everyone headed inside except for Timmy. He was too enthralled as the spider tried to find the perfect spot to create a home for its brood.

When Timmy realized the playground was empty, he stopped to consider that he would probably lose track of the spider if he left. Knowing he was not supposed to take it into the school, he hid it in the only place he could think of—his mouth.

Timmy was late coming in and immediately drew Samantha's attention. She also noticed his big cheeks and the movement inside his mouth. She looked sternly at him and said, "Timmy, you know the rules. Spit out your gum."

Timmy shook his head and spoke through clenched teeth. "I on't ave um."

Samantha could see his mouth was so full he couldn't even speak clearly.

Samantha sighed. "Timmy, do you think I'm stupid? I can see you have gum. Now spit it out."

Timmy shook his head, so Samantha grabbed a tissue from the box on her desk and walked back to him. Holding out her hand, she said, "Spit it out!"

When the spider and all the spit around it hit the tissue, the scream stuck in Samantha's throat. Suddenly, a strange sensation enveloped her, and her world went black. When she came to, she was lying on her back with her children, a couple of teachers, and the principal looking down at her. All the children were there except for Timmy, who was trying to track down his spider.

"Are you okay, Miss Hansen?" Ellen said in a worried voice. The concern showed in the faces of the children.

Samantha tried to get up, but everything was spinning. "I'll cover for you," the principal said. "I think you have had a big shock and should take the rest of the day off."

And that's just what Samantha did.

(Continued)

Teaching and Learning

(Conclusion)

Samantha was embarrassed that she had passed out when Timmy spit the crab spider into her hand. She had wanted to get out of the big city where she grew up and learn what rural life was like. But she was beginning to wonder if she was up to it.

She had learned and seen things she could never imagine. But as the school year was ending, she wondered if she good enough to teach these children.

As the last week of school approached, the principal handed an envelope to each teacher at lunch. When Samantha opened hers, she found a contract for the next school year should she choose to sign it. As she looked at it, the doubt came faster. That was when Mrs. Jensen, the most senior teacher in the school, sat down by her.

"Are you planning to sign up for next year?" Mrs. Jensen asked.

"With all the crazy things I've done this year, I'm really wondering if I'm right for these kids," Samantha replied.

Mrs. Jensen smiled. "I felt the same way after my first year here. And I had my own episode with one of Timmy's family."

"One of his brothers?" Samantha asked.

Mrs. Jensen laughed. "Not way back then. It was his father. He had a giant snake he found on the way to school. He had it zipped in his coat to keep it warm, and it took most of the day to catch it."

"But surely you were used to these things since you grew up here," Samantha said.

"I grew up in the city, just like you," Mrs. Jensen said. "And I almost left after the first year. But the love of the children and the community made me reconsider. I saw you at the community fundraiser for Tanya's dad when he was injured and out of work. You may not know it, but it raised over twenty thousand dollars. And that happens all the time. I decided this was where I wanted to live and raise my family. And I have thousands of other children I count as my own."

They talked a while longer, then the bell rang to go back to class. During the last week, Samantha's class did reports. The children were to write a paper and teach the class about something they were interested in. Most did the minimal one page, and it was usually about something their family did, or a pet. Timmy, of course, wrote about spiders. They were his new fascination. Samantha was surprised that Timmy's paper was many pages long. And except for the grammar, it could have been dissertation material.

The week went by quickly. There was a field trip to a bird refuge followed by a rousing game of kickball. It was boys against girls, with the parents joining the team their child was on. Tanya's dad, the only father to come, almost single-handedly led the girls' team to victory. But in the end, a tie was called so everyone could go home happy.

Too soon, it was the last day of school. After clearing out desks and cleaning, it was time for a party. To keep things clean, the party moved outside, and parents brought lots of delicious treats. It wasn't long before the last bell rang. Samantha slowly followed the children back into the classroom. Her feelings were near the surface, and she wasn't prepared for what happened next.

As the children headed out the door, each one brought her a gift or a handmade note thanking her for being their teacher. The memory of waking up after passing out came to her. She remembered looking up into the faces of the worried children—her children. That was the first time she had thought of them as her own.

As her thoughts returned to the present, she realized there were two children still there. One was Timmy and one was his little sister.

The little sister smiled. "I get to be in your class next year, and Timmy says you're the best teacher ever." Timmy set something on her desk, then ran and gave Samantha a hug, then the two children left.

Samantha hardly dared look at what he left, afraid it might be a spider. Eventually, she looked and she found there was a beautiful blue stone with a note. It was apparent the stone meant a lot to Timmy. When she opened the note, she read the rough handwriting, "Thanks for being my teacher. You're the best!"

When her tears had subsided enough she could see, she cleared a space on her desk, pulled out the contract, and signed it.

A Friend and an Assignment

I made a new friend this summer, and how we met was quite interesting.

I have been working on building a shop on some new property we purchased. We hope to build the shop and move our belongings into it so we can sell our house. Then we will have the money we need to build a new house.

The day I first met Aaron, I was putting up a mailbox. We needed the address and info out on the street to help direct trucks dropping off building supplies. We had a few get mixed up from Google maps and turn onto the road that ran along the side of the canal.

As I was digging the hole for the mailbox, Aaron came riding up on his bicycle and stopped. I said hello, but he didn't answer for a minute. He was wearing a helmet unlike any I had seen before. It was bigger than most bicycle helmets, more like one for a motorcyclist, yet still different.

Eventually, Aaron took off his helmet and said hello. He wanted to know what I had in mind for the property.

"Since you're putting in a mailbox, I presume you plan to move here?" he said in a questioning tone.

"That's the goal," I said. I then explained how we needed to move our belongings and clear our house first to sell it. He told me where he lived, and we both rested as we talked.

From then on, Aaron stopped often. It was almost always the same time of the day, and I would take a needed break from moving dirt and rock or similar challenging work. But then, I noticed Aaron started arriving at my gate an hour later than usual.

One day I asked, "Aaron, do you just go bike riding every day at the same hour or two time range?"

Aaron shrugged. "Yes and no. I do, but not by choice."

He then told me he works in a federal government job. The people he works with are spread out all over the country, and they have to meet each day to coordinate what they have done and what they still need to do.

"We had been meeting remotely using Zoom long before Covid," Aaron said. "But when Covid broke out, my boss, a progressive type of guy, changed things."

Aaron went on to say that they met one day, and the boss said he had been reading reports from the CDC and other places about those who were least affected by the Covid virus.

"It seems that a person has a better chance of survival from Covid when they have high levels of vitamin D and are not obese," the boss said. "So, I decided I need to do something for all of us to get better prepared to ward off the virus. We have all been doing the exact wrong thing by sitting lazily inside. From now on, everyone is to be outside in the sun, exercising while communicating in the meeting."

Aaron said that the boss allocated funds for people to get equipment that would allow them to be outside exercising in whatever way they wanted and still communicate. Aaron got the helmet so he could bike during the meeting, and he liked to adjust his ride so he would end the meeting just as he arrived at my gate. That way we could visit and rest.

"I noticed as the summer wore on, you started arriving an hour later," I said. "I assume your boss moved the time an hour so you could be out in the sun when it was at a better angle?"

Aaron shook his head. "No, the boss had threatened that if everyone didn't work out hard enough during the hour meeting, he would make the meetings two hours long." Then, with sweat still dripping down his face, he said, "The reason I'm an hour later is some people didn't believe him."

I laughed. "Whatever it takes to beat Covid, I guess."

Wide Awake

When I was going to college, I worked as a carpet cleaner. I worked every Saturday and part-time on the days I was at school. The company often forwarded the phone to ours so Donna, my wife, could schedule the appointments for all the carpet cleaners.

There were no cell phones in those days, so I would call Donna to find out my schedule for the evening when I finished my classes. Sometimes, after a long day of classes and homework, it was hard to think about cleaning carpets late into the evening.

One particular day, I had had a lot of classes and a couple of mind-numbing tests. I was exhausted, and the last thing I wanted to do was to clean carpets. But I went to the university courtesy phone and made the call.

Donna answered and told me the appointments. She listed three jobs, all of which were homes requiring cleaning under furniture. For an extra fee, the company had us employees move furniture. It could be backbreaking work, and the only extra pay we got for it was the added hours it took to do the job.

"Aren't there any jobs that don't require me to move furniture?" I asked.

"There is one," she replied. "It's your last one, a gun ammo company. But it also means you're going to have to work a late night. It will be a long job, and they need you to come after the company closes at eight."

I sighed. The only thing worse than moving furniture was working late. I had been up since five in the morning studying for the tests, and I needed some sleep. I had to tell myself that eight wasn't horrible. At least I wasn't cleaning a restaurant after they closed at midnight. I had done that many times.

I went to a school bathroom, changed into my work clothes, and drove to my first job. The people were elderly and could not help. By the time I finished that job, my muscles were already complaining.

The second job was similar, and the third was worse. The lady had a cat, and when I moved the furniture, the carpet under quite a few of them had become a litter box. Under some of them, most of the carpet had rotted away.

When the lady saw it, she picked up her cat and, in a baby voice, said, "Has Esmerelda been a naughty kitty?"

I thought, "Yes. My nose told me that the minute I stepped in the front door."

When I finished each job, if the customer would let me, I would borrow their phone to have Donna inform the next customer I was on my way. By the time I finished, I was running late. To no avail, I had spent extra time trying to get the urine smell out of the carpet.

"The secretary is waiting for you at the gun ammo company," Donna said. Then, with concern in her voice, she asked, "Are you okay?"

"Just super tired," I replied.

"Don't fall asleep driving," she replied.

All the way to the next job, I talked out loud and even slapped my face to stay awake. When I got there, I pulled the equipment out of the truck and made my way to the office.

The secretary pointed to a big oak door, and with a grin on her face, she said, "You're going to clean the company owner's office."

I opened the door, and there stood an enormous Kodiak bear towering over me, ready to strike. I dropped my equipment and fell flat on my back in surprise. The secretary was laughing, and I realized that the bear was stuffed. My heart was pounding so hard it felt like it would break my ribs.

The secretary wiped the tears of mirth from her eyes. "I love to do that."

I cleaned the carpets, and at around eleven, when I finished, I called Donna.

"Are you awake enough to drive?" she asked.

"Believe me," I replied, "I'm not only awake enough to drive, but with the adrenalin that's still in my system, I'll probably be awake all night."

Waking the Dead

I recently I had a chance to do a reader's theatre for a group interested in western history. The stories were a lot of fun, taken from the journals of past residents of the valley where we live. But there was one that I thought was particularly good that goes well with this time of year.

The story was written in the journal of a girl I'll call Laura, who was a teenager at the time. She lived in a small western town, and to earn money to help her family, she hired out as a domestic servant for a wealthy family. After preparing supper for them, she cleaned up and washed the dishes. It was usually quite late when she headed home.

Her walk home took her quite near the town cemetery, but not being a believer in ghosts, that didn't bother her at all. But one moonlit night, well after dark, she was on her way home when she heard something. She was just passing the cemetery when, suddenly, there was a loud commotion. She could see figures dressed in black moving at full speed across the graveyard. Some of them seemed to be falling over tombstones, only to rise up and move even faster.

It was an eerie scene in the dark and it looked like they were almost flying up and down as they ran. Laura felt a little chill, but she reasoned that it couldn't be ghosts. Surely if ghosts did exist, they wouldn't make nearly as much noise. She told herself it was just a bunch of kids playing around, and she was not about to let it frighten her.

But then something did frighten her. In fact, it scared

her so much, she couldn't run if she had wanted to. Coming toward her, almost floating, was a figure dressed in what looked like a white nightgown. The figure continued toward Laura, stopping only a few feet from her. Then Laura recognized who it was, and that frightened her even more. The woman's name was Rachel. She had just passed away a few days before, and her funeral had been that very day. She had been buried that same afternoon.

The woman stood there briefly, staring at Laura in the moonlight as if trying to determine who she was. Then she smiled and spoke.

"Laura, what are you doing out here so late?"

She didn't sound like a ghost, and Laura found her voice. "I just finished work, and I am on my way home. The big question is, what you are doing out here?"

"I had the strangest thing happen," Rachel replied. "I was having a strange dream. Then I woke up. Some men were trying to cut my finger and pull my ring off. I sat up and realized I was down in some hole in the ground. I started to say something to the men, but they scampered away so fast that they didn't even help me out of the hole."

Rachel began to tremble and almost fell. "I feel kind of faint. Can you help me get home?"

Laura was trembling herself, but she took Rachel by the arm and helped her walk. When they arrived at Rachel's house, her husband and children were shocked to see her and a little bit scared at first. But everyone was soon overjoyed, realizing Rachel was very much alive. Laura went to get the doctor.

The doctor checked Rachel thoroughly and said she must have just been in a coma when she was buried. She had obviously come out of it when the grave robbers cut her finger. He suggested they get her some food. Laura helped the family prepare soup, which Rachel slowly, gratefully ate.

Over the next few days, when she wasn't working for the wealthy family, Laura came to help cook and take care of Rachel. Rachel's husband was so overjoyed to have his wife back that he decided to offer a reward to the grave robbers who had brought her out of her coma. He even posted an ad about it in the paper.

But no one ever claimed it.

Running Out of. . .

A bunch of us were visiting at a community picnic years ago. As we did, Jason, a young man in our community, seemed quite melancholy. "What's the matter?" someone asked.

"Dad is a bit miffed at me," Jason replied.

I knew Jason well, and I figured if his dad was only a bit miffed, then it couldn't be as bad as some things he had done in the past.

"What's he miffed about?" I asked.

He then shared the story. He said that his dad had gotten a new tractor, so he invited his friends over to see it.

"Wow!" one boy said. "It's a nice tractor."

"Yeah," Jason told them. "It's got two hundred and fifty horsepower. This baby will pull about anything."

"What are the wide wheels for?" another boy asked.

"It's the latest thing on new tractors," Jason replied. "Those are to help it not get stuck. They spread out across more ground, so the tractor won't sink as easily in a muddy field. This tractor just floats on top."

"I'd love to see that," the boy said. "Do you think it would be okay if we took it for a spin?"

Jason knew he should probably ask, but he was sure the answer would be no if he did. The other boys all looked so hopeful that he just couldn't disappoint them.

"I'm sure dad wouldn't mind if we took it for a little drive," Jason replied.

The boys all stuffed into the cab. Jason started the engine, shifted it into gear, and eased up on the clutch. They started out slow, but it was so fun driving such a powerful machine that it wasn't long before he pulled the throttle wide open. They bounced across the field, through small ditches, and out into the pasture.

In the pasture was a muddy bog. When they came near it, one boy said, "Let's see this baby float across that."

Jason thought for one brief moment that it wasn't a good idea. But all the boys were cheering him on. His single sensible thought quickly left him, as it often does with young men influenced by peer pressure. He gunned the tractor forward and headed straight for the bog. He thought with enough momentum, he would surely make it through.

But the farther they went, the more the wheels spun, and the momentum decreased. Finally, right about the middle of the bog, the tractor stalled with mud up to its axle.

Jason knew his dad would ground him for the rest of his life. When he expressed that sentiment, the others agreed and thought they might not fare too well, either.

"Let's go get your older tractor and pull it out before he can find out," one boy said.

That sounded like a good idea, so they walked the half mile back to the equipment yard where the old tractor was. They got a chain out of the shop, tossed it on the tractor, and all climbed aboard. When they got to the bog, Jason backed up to the mud. The chain wouldn't quite reach, so he kept backing up. Finally, they were able to connect it.

Jason got on the new tractor, and one of the other boys drove the old one. But the old tractor didn't move at all. Its wheels just spun down until the mud was up to its axle. One of the other boys volunteered his dad's tractor, and the result was the same. Another boy brought his dad's tractor, and it, too, got stuck. No one had any more ideas, and they didn't have any more chains.

It was about then that Jason's dad showed up. He looked dumbfounded at the line of tractors chained together.

"Uh, Dad," Jason meekly said, "we're out of chains."

"Chains, nothin'!" his dad said. "It looks like the entire community is out of tractors!"

"And that," Jason told us, "was why his dad was miffed."

Picture Hunting

✦

Bill, a friend of mine from Nebraska, works for a newspaper there. He shared a story that occurred around this time of year.

Bill's assignment at the paper is to follow up on any story that is called in. He specializes in photography, so he is always assigned to ones that might have a good picture involved. One day a call came to the paper about a flock of Sandhill cranes.

"They are beautiful," the caller said. "There are a lot of them, maybe hundreds. I was able to sneak up quite close and get a fantastic view."

The caller said the cranes were up near a local lake in the area. The secretary wrote down all the information and relayed the message to Bill.

Sandhill cranes often stop over in Nebraska in the fall, but not usually in that area. It would be a newsworthy sight to see them there, especially in those numbers. Bill was excited to get a good photograph and write a story for the paper.

When he got to the lake, there were indeed a huge number of birds. But Bill knew immediately that they were not Sandhill cranes. They were far too white. He figured they might be snow geese. And even though they weren't as rare in that area, there were so many of them that they would still make an excellent picture and story. The picture should be as good as that of cranes, maybe better.

Bill wanted the perfect shot, so he started sneaking up on the birds. The going was not the easiest, carefully picking his way through the brush, but he was used to doing such things for his stories. He spent a long time, carefully working his way closer to the birds. But then, something made him reconsider what he was seeing. He was close enough to see their movements, but none seemed to be doing anything.

Bill pulled out his binoculars and had a good look. Sure enough, the birds were immobile. That was when he noticed that some were even in the act of taking off, but they, too, didn't move. All the birds were decoys. But they were excellent decoys. They had fooled him and the person who had called the newspaper. And to add to that, there were hundreds of them. Usually, when a person sets out decoys, there are only a few.

Bill wondered why so many had been set out. Was it hunters or birders trying to draw snow geese in? But why would they need so many?

Bill debated taking a picture of them and trying to make a story, but he felt a little sheepish knowing he had spent so much time sneaking up on fakes. But he still wanted to have a picture he could take home.

Bill knew there were some eagles and real snow geese in the area, so he went in search of them. Eventually, he found some eagles and got some beautiful pictures. As he was returning past the site of the decoys, he saw some movement among them. There were some men dressed in white walking between the decoys.

Bill thought this was his big chance. He could talk to the men and solve the mystery of why they had set out so many. He slowed his car, but something stopped him from talking to the men. Between him and where the men were was a pasture full of mean-looking bulls. He was curious about the birds, but he wasn't interested enough to cross that field. So, Bill turned and headed home, a beautiful picture of an eagle on his camera for his news story.

And the mystery of the many decoys at the lake remained a mystery.

Fast-Attack Volleyball

My mother is ninety-five and lives in an assisted living center. The people in charge there provide a lot of activities for the residents to enjoy. There are, of course, things like card games, Bingo, and putting puzzles together. My mother doesn't get too excited about any of those. She grew up as a hard-working farm girl, and playing Bingo just isn't in the cards for her.

But there are other, even more far-reaching activities. One of the owners has a pond that he stocks with fish. The residents go in a van to the pond, then fish from lawn chairs on the dock. Some young people even bait their hooks for them.

Mom never did like fishing. My father, brothers, and some of my sisters enjoyed it, and we would go when we could. Mom would go with us and take a book to read.

The assisted living center has had outings to parks, short hikes on trails that were wheelchair accessible, and long rides to see the countryside. My Mom has gone on a few but usually comes back and says, "If you've seen it once, there's no need to see it again."

I have been concerned about her being bored, so I have provided her with all the crossword puzzle books I can get my hands on. She enjoys them. But with her eyesight fading, that is becoming increasingly difficult.

There was one thing she found she enjoyed. It was called M&M night. The M's stand for music and movies. They had someone come in and play music for old silent films. A person could win M&M's if they could guess the piece of music that the lady was playing. I was pleased to see that my mother had a whole bowl full of M&M's.

But one day, I was surprised to hear my mother talking about the residents playing a rousing volleyball game. She was telling me how much fun she had.

"Some players are incredibly aggressive," she said. "The lady next to me kept getting in my road when I tried to hit the ball. Everyone has to keep reminding people to stay in their own areas."

I was shocked to think of my mother playing volleyball at her age. She has said she wanted to get more exercise, but I was concerned that it might push her heart a little too much. When I asked her about it, she brushed it off.

"No," she replied. "I do just fine, and I make sure I get my fair share of shots. My team ended up winning three of the five games. And a couple of the times, I was the one that made the winning hit across the net."

She was proud of the excellent job she did, and I was pleased she found something she enjoyed. But the more she talked about it, the more shocked I was. Still, I tried not to show my angst for her. I didn't want to say anything that would deter her from doing the things she liked.

There were a couple more times that she played volleyball, and every time, she had to tell me about the games. She said her team was even getting so they would set the ball for each other so the people on the front could slam it.

By this time, I was so perplexed about her playing volleyball that I took some time off work to come see the next match. When I got there, I found the tables in the cafeteria scooted to the sides. A net between three and four feet high divided the room. All the residents sat in chairs on their side of the net. A worker launched a ball-shaped balloon out into their midst, and the residents started smacking it back and forth with paddles.

When the match was over, I told Mom she hadn't described the low net, the balloon ball, the chairs, the paddles, or any of that.

She looked at me with disgust. "Why should I? What else would we be doing?"

I thought of what I had imagined and smiled. "It doesn't matter as long as you were having fun."

Smokin' Hot Cookin'

Rihanna loved to cook, and everyone loved her namesake dishes, especially when she made Italian cuisine. Her spices were strong, and the flavor was powerful. Her husband, Steven, always praised her creations. His mother did, too, saying that Rihanna's Italian cooking was the best in the world. That is something a mother-in-law might be reticent to admit.

But Rihanna had one weakness. She liked to smoke. "Liked to smoke" is probably not the correct phrase. She was a chain smoker, and though she had tried to break the habit many times, she had not prevailed.

Steven worried about Rihanna's health. Even though she was only in her early forties, she had developed a constant cough that was getting worse. He insisted she go to the doctor and have it checked. The doctor's diagnosis wasn't a surprise. The smoking was causing Rihanna health problems, and she needed to quit.

With encouragement from family and friends, Rihanna quit. She had gone without a cigarette for more than a month when she realized something: smoking had affected her sense of taste. Rihanna had never really followed a recipe, just making everything to taste. But smoking had apparently dulled some of her senses. Now that she wasn't smoking, she was more sensitive to different flavors. She started reducing both the types and amounts of the spices she was putting in her well-known dishes.

Suddenly, no one was raving about her cooking anymore. The final straw came the day her young son told her that something she made was bland. She had never heard of smoking dulling the sense of taste. Maybe it was genetic and was just her. But when she visited with Steven, though he tried to save her feelings, he eventually admitted that her cooking didn't taste the same now.

The next day, when Steven came home, he was shocked to see Rihanna smoking. "I thought you had quit," he said.

Rihanna nodded. "I had. But I want to get my taste back to where it was. Then I will make my favorite dishes the way everyone loves them. But this time, when I get to that point, I will write it all down. Then I can give up smoking and continue to cook the way I did before."

Steven was concerned that this would backfire and get herself hooked again. But there was no way she would change her mind, so he supported her in the decision. And when she started making all her hallmark dishes the way she did before, she carefully measured every ingredient she put in them. Once she had sure, tried-and-true recipes, written and tested, she put away the cigarettes.

Rihanna was true to her word. She never smoked again. She had powerful motivation not to. First, she wanted to make sure she was around to be a mother to her young son. And second, she loved to cook, and she now realized smoking was affecting her sense of taste. Though she knew she might not have made the wonderful dishes she had if she hadn't smoked, she wanted to taste them the way others tasted them.

As her tastebuds returned to their nonsmoking condition, everything she made tasted too spicy, even though everyone else seemed to like it. So she started by making herself a separate portion more in line with her new flavor desires. But she always tried what the others ate. Over time, she grew to like what the others ate more and more. Soon, she only ate what everyone else ate and enjoyed it just like they did.

After a year of her hard work, giving up smoking and working to make and like the food everyone else did, Steven took her in his arms and told her he was grateful that she was willing to work at giving up smoking. He said he wanted her to be with him for a long time. He then presented her with a new plaque for her kitchen.

It said, "If you think the cookin' is smokin' hot, you should meet the cook."

The Quilt

My wife, Donna, wants each of her children and grandchildren to have a beautiful, warm quilt. Over the years, she has made sure our children had one for their bed, one for college, one for their wedding, and one for other times when they needed it. Donna has always said that when they wrapped up in their quilts, they could think about it as if their mother was hugging them.

Now that all of our children are gone from home, her attention has turned to making quilts for our grandchildren. This Thanksgiving, one of our sons brought his family to visit. That was the perfect chance for Donna and our daughter-in-law, Janalyn, to work on some quilts for their two children to replace the baby quilts Donna had made for them. The first opportunity they got, Donna and Janalyn sat down to go through Donna's supply of fabric.

As they were looking at different squares Donna had already cut out, our four-year-old granddaughter came to watch what they were doing. Sometimes Hannah doesn't say too much, but she usually has a way of letting you know what she wants. At one point, Donna pulled out a bigger piece of fabric that she planned to use for another project she was working on. As she set it aside, Hannah's eyes showed her excitement.

The fabric was purple and covered with beautiful, sparkly butterflies. Hannah got up, picked up the material, and left the room. Donna and Janalyn looked at each other, then followed to see what she was doing with it. They found her in the bedroom across the hall and watched as she put the fabric into Janalyn's suitcase.

Hannah knew that her grandma's fabric drawer contained material for quilts for the grandchildren. She must have thought the butterfly piece was a finished quilt, unlike most of the material in the drawer. After watching Hannah's actions, Donna turned to Janalyn.

"Well, I don't think we need to guess what Hannah would like for her quilt."

They waited until Hannah wasn't looking, then retrieved the fabric from the suitcase. It wasn't quite as big as Donna wanted the quilt to be, so she sewed some beautiful purple strips around each side until it formed a full blanket. The challenge was that each time they set it aside for a moment, Hannah would gather it up and put it back in the suitcase.

Finally, the butterfly side was done. Then came the question of what would go on the other side. Donna found a baby shark fabric someone had given her, and Janalyn said that Hannah loved baby shark.

Donna had just finished putting the pieces together with the batting between, when Hannah noticed the butterfly fabric was missing from the suitcase. She came in and saw her grandmother working on it. She had a worried expression on her face as if she was wondering whether it would be hers or not.

Donna took the quilt to the quilting machine. After she fastened it on, she quilted part, and Janalyn quilted the rest, so it could be a gift from both of them. Meanwhile, Hannah didn't let it out of her sight. I couldn't even encourage her to come eat, build a fort with Lincoln logs with me, or anything. She just stood on the couch so she would have a good view to watch her mother and grandmother.

Finally, when the quilt was done, removed from the machine, and bound, the two women presented the little girl with the quilt. Hannah's eyes lit up with excitement, especially when she saw that it also had baby sharks on it.

While Donna and Janalyn made a Baby Yoda quilt for Hannah's little brother, Hannah spent much of the rest of the Thanksgiving weekend wrapped in her quilt. Sometimes she wanted the butterflies to show on the outside, and sometimes she wanted the baby sharks.

And when she brought her blanket to curl up in as she sat by me to watch a movie, I could sense the greatest pleasure she got from it was knowing her mother and grandmother love her.

Naming Chickens

At a recent church social, we got to talking about chickens. It was a strange topic to settle in on as we were socializing, and I thought it would be a dull discussion for the evening. And I'm not even sure how we got there in the first place. I think Julie said something about her husband, Kevin, being retired and not having anything to do. So, she had suggested that he get chickens.

"Chickens definitely did give him something to do," Julie said. "Or more to the point, it gave him something to complain about." She then turned to Kevin and said, "Didn't it, Dear?"

Kevin rolled his eyes. "It's always something. They start molting and quit laying. They decide there is one chicken they don't like, and they all peck at it. It goes on and on."

"Well, I suppose it beats complaining about politics," Sally said. "When my husband gets annoyed with a politician, that might be all I hear about for weeks."

"Do any of you name your chickens?" Carol asked.

"My husband does, and he doesn't," Sally replied. "He told our grandchildren every chicken was named 'Doomed,' and now our youngest granddaughter goes around pointing at each chicken saying, 'You're doomed, and you're doomed, and you're doomed.' The funny thing is, she doesn't understand what she is saying and thinks it's just a name."

"I have never let my children name any of our chickens," I said. "I didn't want them getting too attached to them."

Kevin said he made the mistake of letting one of his granddaughters choose one of the chickens as her own when she stayed with them for the summer. "Next thing I knew, she had it sleeping on her bed with her."

"Kevin's old aunt has a bunch of chickens," Julie said, "and she named every one. They are all pets. When she comes out, they come running because she often has little treats for them."

"And it's not just her they come running to," Kevin said. "They get so underfoot that a person can hardly walk across the yard."

Julie nodded. "His aunt told him that he ought to name his chickens. She said he would like them a lot better if he did."

"I doubt it," Kevin replied. "I'm sure they would taste the same either way."

Julie whacked him playfully. "You know very well that's not what she meant."

"Well, I did name them," Kevin said. "I named them after all the girls I liked in high school. I even named the one rooster I had after the high school quarterback who used to make my life miserable. It kind of seemed appropriate since the rooster doesn't seem to like me very much. I named the prettiest chicken after the girl in high school that I thought was the prettiest."

"I bet it would please her to know that," I replied. "Maybe she would name something of hers after you."

Kevin laughed. "She didn't even know I existed, and she couldn't name anything after me because she didn't even know my name. And if she ever figured out what my name was, she wouldn't name a kickin' jacka . . ."

Julie whacked Kevin again. "Kevin, we're at a church social."

Kevin sighed. "Okay. She wouldn't name a. . . um, a dad-blamed donkey after me."

I laughed. Maybe chickens were an interesting topic of conversation after all.

End of Semester Questions

Students often ask interesting questions. Many of these occur at the end of the semester as the grades are approaching finalization. Maybe some of the strangeness of their questions come from the added stress of wrapping up everything. But I thought I'd include a few of the questions.

1. Professor Howard, would you mind explaining something? We have had two tests, and I don't think they are weighted the same. I got 70% on the first one and was very pleased. I have never done that well at math. When the second test came, I decided that I wouldn't worry about taking it since I had done so well on the first one. But now my test average shows as 35%. I think the passing test must not be weighted as much because the non-passing test made my grade so I am failing. Why would my failing test be counted more than my passing test?

My answer: All the tests are weighted equally. If you take the average of seventy and zero, it is thirty-five. You need to take all tests and not skip one.

2. Hi Professor Howard. I have a question for you. Is the final a test? You said one test would be dropped, so I didn't worry about taking the unit three exam. But my grade has fallen to failing, and the only places I see a problem are the zero in test three and the one in the final.

My answer: Yes, the final is a test. You should note that I said I drop one of the *four* tests. I put the zero in the final so you could see your actual grade all semester. Some people who have done well on the other three don't take it, but it looks like you will need to. By the way, it closes tomorrow.

3. (This is from one of my computer science students.) Professor Howard, I have a question that is driving me crazy. I have a friend that thinks the world is all about Apple products. His dad has an old iMac he still uses. My friend has had every version of iPod that Apple has made. His dad gave him an iBook when we were both young. He, of course, has an iPhone and an iPad. He calls his watch an iWatch, even though I don't think that is what it is really called. But recently, he has talked about Safari this and Safari that until I finally asked what Safari was. Well, it is the name of the Apple browser. He acted like I was really naive for not knowing that. But my question is, seriously, what is the deal with their naming scheme if they only follow it half the time? The obvious choice for the browser would be iBrowse, and then a person would know for sure what it was.

My Answer: Maybe they were afraid people would mistake it for eye brows.

4. (From one of my English majors.) Dear Professor Howard, I write you now because, after three hours of cognitive thought, the calculations to my 4F Math Problems have yet to solidify in my gelatinous mind. My desperate hope is for a planned, or even chance, meeting with you, where I could bask in the aura of your infinite wisdom to cure me of my mathematical frailties. If it is conceivably possible that we could meet tomorrow (Friday) at your office (or another place of your choosing), I would greatly appreciate your sacrifice. However, if you do not wish to plan to meet with me... I beg that you might tell me of your general whereabouts, in the which I hope I might randomly run into you. If

you do not wish to be found, you can either not clue me in to your whereabouts or simply choose to be elsewhere. As a result, I will be saddened but will inevitably get over it. Thank you for the precious commodity of time you used to read this email.

My answer: Sure, we can meet. How about 10:15 at my office?

Santa Claus

I've read that people playing Santa are in short supply this year. I know that the people who usually ask me have not requested any visits. I've seen a few Santas out and about, but they have been few. I wonder if Covid has affected both those wanting to have Santa come, and those wishing to play the part.

We were planning to visit my daughter this week, so she asked if I could play Santa for her kids. "They missed out on it last year with Covid," she said, "and the people in charge of our community celebration didn't schedule anyone to come play Santa there like they usually do."

I was free of Covid, so I told her I would be happy to do that for my grandchildren. She called again a few hours later and said she had mentioned it to some of her friends. She said they asked if they could join us. I told her that would be fine. Then, a few hours later, she called once more.

"I was visiting with one of the ladies in charge of our community party, and she said the only reason we weren't having Santa there was because we couldn't find anyone to do it."

My daughter asked me if I would do it for the entire neighborhood. I told her I'd be happy to.

At the party, we found most people there still assumed Santa wasn't coming, but a few parents had found out.

"With Covid and everything, I'm not sure anyone even thinks about Santa anymore," one mother said. "I know my teenage son only does to go on and on about how silly it is to believe in Santa."

Comments like that made me wonder how it would turn out. After everyone finished eating, they started singing Christmas songs. I slipped out to don my Christmas clothes and change into my alter ego persona. It wasn't long before my wife signaled it was time for me to enter.

As I ho-hoed my way into the hall, jingling the bells, the entire crowd burst into joyous and loud applause. Immediately, the children came to greet me, with a few teenagers in the lead.

"So, what's my name?" a young teenage boy asked with a sly smile.

"Are you serious?" I replied. "You don't even know your name? I bet if you asked your mom, she could help you with that."

The other teenagers laughed, and one said, "I think he's beyond help."

They ushered me to a chair they had prepared. I had requested someone to indirectly let me know the children's names. The lady chosen was good. As the same boy came to visit with me, the lady said, "Okay, Josh, we're read. Go ahead."

He let out a sigh. Now he couldn't try the same trick. So, he changed his approach. Grinning, he asked, "Where are your reindeer? I don't see them outside anywhere."

"This time of year, they are resting, taking vitamins, and getting strong for the big day coming up," I replied. "I can't be wearing them out on a trip like this when they have such an important night next week."

The boy gasped in exasperation, and the other teenagers laughed. But he wasn't through with me yet.

"So, how did you get here?" he asked.

"Have you heard of United Airlines?" I replied.

"There are no airlines at the North Pole," he said.

"No," I said. "That's why I have to take a little commuter snow-plane down to Anchorage."

By now the smaller children were clamoring for a turn. That and the good-natured ribbing of his friends seemed to halt his plan, so he took his candy cane and went on his way. But he and his friends were back later for rounds two, three, and more. But luckily, each time, I had an answer to their questions.

Later, an older person pulled me aside. "That was quick thinking with those teenagers," he said. "Maybe that's why so few people play Santa."

I actually thought the challenge with the teenagers was fun. But what always brought me back to play Santa again and again were the requests from the children that touched my heart.

(Continued.)

Santa Claus

(Conclusion)

I've only seen a few people playing Santa this year, and they were paid. I like to do it for the enjoyment, and being paid diminishes that for me. So, when my daughter asked me to play Santa for her children, then later asked instead for her entire community, I agreed.

Most people at the community dinner didn't think Santa was coming and seemed disappointed. So they seemed happy when they learned the news. "I have a shy little five-year-old daughter," a lady said. "She would love to see Santa, but not having had the chance for almost two years, I think she will be too scared."

The shy little girl came and nervously asked for music from the movie *Frozen*. When I asked which one, she said both. "But could you make it easy piano music because I'm just learning to play?" We then talked about playing piano, and with a nod from her mother, I told her to look for the music on Christmas.

There were the normal rambunctious teenagers, and then there were some, as always, that touched my heart. A rebelliously dressed teenaged boy said he just wanted his dad to come home. And at the end of the line, waiting patiently and quietly until everyone else was done, was a little boy about six years old. Through the evening, I had just pulled the children close to stand by me, afraid the parents would be concerned about them sitting on my lap because of Covid. But he asked specifically if he could sit on my lap and give me a hug. I looked at his mother for permission, and she nodded.

I pulled him onto my lap, and after a big hug, asked him what he wanted for Christmas. He said, "All I want for Christmas is for my parents to get back together so we can be a family again."

My heart melted. I told him I was sure they loved him, but sometimes adults don't agree on things. Then I said, "But there is one other thing I want you to always remember when things get hard. I want you to know I love you."

His mother cried, and the boy hugged me again before smiling and taking his candy cane. I turned and looked at the line. It started filling up with children who had already visited with me. I thought maybe they saw I still had more candy canes or forgot a request the first time. But when I asked the first little girl if she wanted another piece of candy, she shook her head.

"Nope. I just came to climb on your lap and get a hug like Kevin did."

And that was true of all of them, though a few accepted a second treat. But what they really wanted was a hug. When they all had gotten their hug, some of them more than one, I shared the left-over candy canes with the parents.

When I had finished and went to change back to the normal me, I thought about what had just happened. Sometimes children ask me if Santa is real. I thought, "Oh, he's real, all right. And he's part of all of us, whether it is when we need a hug or have an extra one to share."

I also thought of what we have lost through this last year. The children yearned for love, a hug, and a feeling of approval. I was Covid free, so I could feel comfortable being close to the children. But some people asked if I wasn't afraid of catching Covid by playing Santa. I answered that I wasn't scared of getting it. Yes, I know I could lose my life. But what I am really afraid of is losing something more important: humanity, charity, and compassion.

This last year, we have seen an increase in anger, hatred, prejudice, and mistrust. Some have promoted it for their own gain to the detriment of others. The youngest members of our society are the most sensitive, and I feel it affects them the most, especially when the normalcy we so desperately seek seems so far away.

The children there touched my heart and made me consider what is most important. The experience made me commit to looking more for good in others, lift someone who could use a kind word, and try to make someone else's life a little better.

Corgi Capital of the World

Jed and Nicole were annoyed with each other. They had had their marital disagreements in the past, but this one seemed to be growing way out of proportion. It had started when Jed said he didn't believe something Nicole read to him from the internet.

"Look," Jed said, "you can't trust everything you read on the internet, even on Wikipedia. The good people there attempt to have policies and procedures to make articles as true as possible. I appreciate them and have donated to them. But people still make mistakes. And besides, there are few bad actors who post false things on purpose."

"I think you are just too skeptical," Nicole replied. "I feel if something is posted on a site like Wikipedia, it can even be quoted as fact for research."

Jed knew that arguing with his wife further on the subject was futile. When her mind was made up, the only way to change it was with irrefutable proof. That thought gave Jed an idea. He would create the evidence needed to convince his wife.

Jed sat down with his computer and created a Wikipedia account. He used a nickname that people had used for him when he was young because he didn't want everyone knowing his identity. Now he had to come up with an article. He wanted it to be benign enough that no one would pay attention to it. But it had to be believable so his wife would think it was true.

He thought for a long time, but nothing seemed quite right. Then their little corgi dog named Bess came and laid her head on his leg, wanting some attention. As he reached down to pet her, he suddenly had an idea. He typed and typed, adding in false facts, some free pictures from the internet, and a picture of his own.

When he finished, he edited and re-edited the article until he thought it was perfect, then submitted it. He would have to wait until it was up on the site. Then he would give it a whole week so he could tell Nicole it had been there for a while. That's when he would show her.

It didn't take long before Jed could verify that the article was live. He felt pretty smug seeing it there. It was going to be a long week before he could prove his point to his wife. He decided the following Sunday evening would be the perfect time to casually tell her. Meanwhile, he was sure it wouldn't be a problem that he posted it because no one would even notice it.

The following Sunday, when he arrived at church, he was walking down the hall outside the chapel when he heard a group of older people talking.

"Did you see the article in the paper this morning about the fame that has come to our little town?" one old gentleman asked.

"You mean how Greenville is the corgi capital of the world?" a woman replied.

The man nodded. "More corgis per capita than any other town in the world."

Jed spun around. "Did you say there was an article about Greenville corgis in the paper?"

"Yes," the woman said. "We even have a small park donated by a dedicated corgi owner that is just for corgis, and no other breeds of dogs are allowed. I'm not sure where it is, but the paper talked about it."

"That's the dumbest thing I ever heard," another man said. "In my day, we had sensible sheep herding dogs."

"But do you really believe the article?" Jed said, hoping to throw some brakes on this disaster.

"Well, of course," the second man said. "The newspaper said it was in Wikipedia."

Jed hurried home after church and read the paper. Sure enough, there was the headline, "Greenville, Corgi Capital of the World." Maybe if he hurried, he could get it off before Nicole saw it. But when she walked in carrying the newspaper and shouting, "Have you seen the news?!" he knew he was too late.

It took him a while to confess what he had done and even longer to convince her. He had to show her it was his nickname on the article, and one picture was of a neighbor's corgi and Bess.

"So, you're one of those deceptive people you were talking about?" she said in disgust.

"I'm just trying to prove a point," he replied.

"What are you going to do now that everyone thinks it's real?" Nicole asked.

Jed thought a minute, and then even though Nicole advised against it, he decided he might add to the article and see if the town's people caught on.

(Continued)

Still the Corgi Capital of the World

Jed had created a Wikipedia site claiming their little town was the corgi capital of the world. He said they had more corgi dogs per capita than any other place. He did it to show his wife, Nicole, that not everything on the internet is factual. But when the paper picked it up, and it became big news in their small community, he decided not to back down or admit his culpability.

"Maybe I can educate others in this town, too," he said to Nicole.

Nicole rolled her eyes. "You'll just make yourself look stupid."

He had already posted that they had a special park just for corgis, and no other animals were allowed. He would have to come up with another interesting item. But as he was adding things, something else happened that he didn't expect.

Someone, who claimed to be from a town halfway around the world, said Jed was wrong, and his city was the corgi capital of the world. The person had added all sorts of things to Jed's page. Suddenly, this was not an education initiative—it was war.

The stranger said they had a unique club in their town just for corgi owners. Jed countered, saying his town not only had a club but a special holiday. The stranger said they had a special day each year when everyone with corgis could walk down the street with their dogs. He said it was a spectacular parade. Not to be outdone, Jed claimed Greenville had a dog contest just for corgis. The stranger said that they not only had a contest, but a fair where the well-trained corgis could show off their skills at their owner's commands.

Nicole shook her head when she saw what was happening. "You come home from work at night, and the first thing you do is login to your account to see if that person has topped you. And who knows if he is telling the truth any more than you are."

"I put a lot of truth on there," Jed complained. "I talk about where the breed came from, what its name means, and many other things. And I don't really lie; I just stretch the facts."

"You only tell enough truth that the people will believe your fable narrative," Nicole said.

Jed had to admit that maybe this was all getting out of hand. He had visited with a friend about it, and his friend said, "Interpretation of facts only stretch so far, then they break. And when they break, they turn into outright lies."

Jed thought maybe he should remove the false stuff on his page, even though he knew Nicole would claim she was right about things on the internet being true. But before he could remove the false claims, both his and the stranger's accounts were suspended, and the page was removed.

If he thought she would say she was right before, there was nothing like now. "See, they took down your account because you were posting false things. That's why I trust them, because they see through little charades like yours."

But they only suspended his and the stranger's account for a short time for being a bit terse with each other. And when the accounts came back on, and the page was restored, Jed decided it was time to end his experiment. He deleted all the false things he had written on the page. Much to his surprise, after he had deleted his stuff that wasn't true, the stranger deleted most of his material, too. Maybe the stranger was making up stuff as well.

And Nicole said to Jed, "I still trust most of what I read on internet sites like Wikipedia." Then with a smile she added, "Unless you wrote it."

(Author's disclaimer: Though the story was written about an actual event, the names, and even the animal type, were changed to protect the not-so innocent. Also, no animals were harmed in the making of this story.)

Children and Phone Calls

I think anyone who has had children has had a time when a child has embarrassed them. I know we have. My wife, Donna, had such an experience with one of our sons.

She was on a very important phone call where she was connected with a group of people reviewing theatre scripts. Some of these people were famous authors. Others were well-known actors. Donna felt a little inferior in the group. She had timidly given a few of her thoughts on the selections being considered, but she didn't want to insert her suggestions into the meeting too much.

Everything was going well when our son, who was only about five, came to her.

"Mommy," he said, "I want to show you what I have learned to do."

Donna covered the mouthpiece of the phone. "Honey, Mommy is on a very important phone call right now. Could it wait until later?"

Our little son nodded and went on his way. About five minutes later, he came back. "Mommy, it's later. Do you want to know what I learned now?"

Once more, Donna covered the receiver. "Mommy is going to be a little bit longer. But I promise you can show me the minute I'm done."

He left and was gone only a few minutes this time before he was back. Since she said she would let him show her what he had learned when she finished, he impatiently waited. He just stared at her, sighing heavily now and then.

Finally, Donna turned to him to signal that they were finishing up the phone call, and she would be done in just a minute. But there were two problems with that. She couldn't signal to him and cover the phone at the same time, and he took the signal to mean that she was ready for his demonstration.

With that, he let out a belch that just about shook the house and would have made a tugboat horn feel inferior. Suddenly, everyone on the phone call went completely silent. Finally, an older lady said, "Well, I guess someone feels better."

Donna was sure they must have thought it was her, so she tried to explain, but it was hard for anyone to believe that came from a five-year-old.

The next week, the group was conducting a conference call to finalize the selection. Donna made sure the young children were fed and had lots of toys to play with. She hoped that would keep them busy so there wouldn't be a repeat of the previous week's episode.

When the conference call came, Donna sat down at the bottom of the stairs. This week, there were lots of questions for her. She had the most expertise in musical theatre, and the others wanted to know her opinion on some musical options. She was deep into the conversation when she felt something brush against her face. She turned, and there, dangling by her, was a snake.

She let out a scream that could have wakened Rip Van Winkle from his slumber.

"Mommy," our little boy said, "I found the toy snake."

As Donna sat there panting from the fright she had received, there were lots of voices on the phone. They were asking if she was all right. After she explained what had happened, the same lady that had the sarcastic comment the week before said, "Well, I am now officially deaf."

"Oh, come on," someone else replied. "Haven't you had a child do something like that to you?"

"No," the lady replied. "I am single, and I plan to stay that way."

Donna was embarrassed. But that night, as we gathered for our family story and singing time, our little son cuddled up in his mother's lap.

She smiled. "All the embarrassment and scares in the world are worth it for this."

Children and Grandchildren

It was a Saturday, and I was home from school and work. My wife, Donna, was off to an activity with some other women, so I was taking care of our two-year-old daughter, Celese. She was our only child, but we were expecting another one soon. I had been working on some homework when I heard a knock on the door.

When I opened it, there stood an older lady who was a friend of Donna's. The lady wanted to make sure we knew she was available to come watch Celese when the new baby came. I told her that Donna was gone, but I expected her back soon.

"Don't be afraid to call me day or night," she kindly said. "And from my experience, these things seem to happen more at night."

We were visiting when I suddenly realized everything was silent. Celese had been playing with some toys in the bedroom, but I wasn't hearing anything. I excused myself to check on her, and I found that she was no longer in the bedroom. In the panic that wraps itself around a parent's heart, especially a new parent, I started dashing around the apartment to find her.

When I got to the kitchen, there she was. Earlier, I had made some bread to surprise Donna. When I had tried to get the lid off the flour bucket, I had to really work at it. I couldn't understand why it was on so tight. I thought maybe we had used the bucket to sit on at the table because of the limited furniture in our college-student furnished apartment. When I put the lid back on the bucket, I had put it on loosely so it would be easier to remove the next time.

You guessed it, Celese was covered from head to toe in flour, and half the kitchen was, too. Suddenly, I realized someone was standing behind me, and when I turned, there was the lady. She gave me a look of pity and talked in a tone of voice that indicated she wondered about my child-watching capability.

"And if you need me at times besides when the baby comes," she said, "don't be afraid to ask."

She was kind, but I was embarrassed, and I was grateful when she left. I then took my little two-year-old ghost to give her a bath.

Celese is grown now and has children of her own. She has one blond, blue-eyed daughter that looks like a perfect angel. She is, most of the time, too. So, when she does something that is less than perfect, it is often a shock to everyone. I smiled as Celese told us what had happened one day.

At the time, Celese's daughter was four. Celese had a group of women over for a meeting about the arts in their community. They were planning some theatre productions and some concerts. These ladies were some of the leading women in the town. Celese was new there and wanted to get involved in some activities these women oversaw.

The women were deep into a conversation about upcoming events. Celese had just served some of her famous chocolate chip cookies and punch, and everyone was remarking about how good they were. It was then that Celese's little angelic daughter stepped into the room.

"Did you need something, sweetie?" Celese asked.

Her little daughter just held up a finger. "Wait for it. Wait for it. Wait for it." Then she let out a long, loud burst of gas. She smiled and said, "Okay, I'm good," and she left.

Celese was more than just a little mortified, especially as the smell wafted their direction. She was sure her status in the community had just dropped off the bottom of the social scale. Not knowing what else to do and wanting to change the subject, Celese held out the plate of cookies. "Another cookie, anyone?"

The oldest, most prominent woman of the group shook her head and put the cookie she was eating down on the table. "No, I'm good."

As Celese told me the story, I thought about a cute little gremlin, flour ghost, and I smiled. As a grandparent, it is always interesting to see our grandchildren give their own parents some of what their parents gave us.

Second Place

This time of year, when wrestling season is ending, I often think back to my days of competition. On our team, our coach's philosophy was that losing wasn't an option. This came across strongly one Monday.

We had just come home the night before from a road trip that had taken the whole week. We had swung up through Montana, wrestling at the most prominent universities. We ended with a tough two-day tournament in Wyoming. Despite the number of matches and the quality of the opponents, Coach said the same thing he always said after competition.

"Now, don't forget that those of you who lost any match this last week owe me a mile of running up and down the stadium stairs."

"Does that include Howard?" Larry asked. "It doesn't seem fair to include him."

"Yeah," Jack added. "His opponents were a little over the top, and he still won all but one of his matches."

Larry was our heavyweight, and Jack was our 170-pound wrestler. They were the two I worked out with during practice and were my best friends on the wrestling team. We had all three faced tough opponents, but Larry and Jack were former national champions and top in their class. They were also older and more experienced than I was.

They were right in that I had drawn some tough competition. Of our three matches against other universities, two of my three opponents had placed at nationals the year before. I had won both of those matches, though they were tough fights to the end. But my last opponent at the Wyoming tournament had been the national champion in my weight class.

Luckily, with the week's wins, I was rated second at the tournament in my weight. So, they put me in the opposite side of the bracket from the national champion. That meant I wouldn't face him until the end if I could keep winning. It also meant my side of the bracket was the tougher side.

I had some tough matches that I pulled out at the very end. One thing I prided myself on was being in good shape and having the stamina to push my opponents hard in the second and third rounds. I had been behind at the end of the first round in some matches but came back to wear out my opponents and pull out wins.

When we got to the championship round on Saturday night, only four from our team were vying for the tournament title in our weights: Jack, Larry, our 110-pound wrestler, and me. Our 110-pound wrestler lost. I was next up from our team and had a tough-fought match. I was down by six after the first round, but I pulled up even by the end of the second. The lead seesawed back and forth between us in the last round, but he pulled out a win with an escape in the last few seconds.

Jack and Larry won, giving our team second in the tournament. Even though that was outstanding for our small college, Coach made it clear that he was not satisfied.

"Howard, if you would have won, we would have barely had enough points for a first place."

So now it was Monday after practice, and Jack and Larry felt it was unfair to expect me to run the extra mile because of my loss.

"Oh, whine, whine, whine," Coach replied to their entreaties on my behalf. "You'd think this was a vineyard with that much whine."

"It's okay, guys," I replied. "It will just make me that much stronger."

"Good attitude, Howard," Coach said. Then, pointing at a poster on the wall, he said, "Don't forget my core philosophy."

Coach had lots of what he called "motivational" posters in the wrestling room. Some of them I consider as doubtful in that capacity. But as I headed out to run my mile, I glanced up at the one he mentioned. I shook my head and sighed a bit as I read it.

It said, "Second place is nothing but a first-place loser."

Valentine Mystery

✦

My daughter, Elliana, was in her first year of high school when she got to see a Valentine's Day tradition there firsthand. Students left notes, hearts, or candy where someone they cared about would find them. This could be on lockers, a classroom desk, a car, or anywhere else they knew the right person would come across it.

Some were precursors to a hopeful date invitation. But many didn't have the desired effect, especially if the person giving it was too shy to sign their name. Others were not even manifestations of romantic love. Some were simply notes of friendship or pictures to inspire and uplift them on this day.

Elliana had a big group of friends, and many of them gave Valentines to each other. One girl in the group, Sarah, especially liked Tyson, a guy in the group. Sarah worked hard to make the perfect Valentine, then enlisted Elli's help to post it on Tyson's locker. Elli and Sarah then hid to see what he would do when he saw it.

To Sarah's dismay, Tyson approached his locker carrying a card bigger than the one she had made. She was disappointed and wanted to leave, but Elli talked her into at least talking to him. As the two girls approached, he seemed to be staring with concern at the card.

"Is something the matter?" Sarah asked.

Tyson nodded. "Look at this Valentine on my locker. I'm sure it's from Amy."

Elli could see the disappointment on Sarah's face that he hadn't guessed it was from her. Sarah looked like she would cry, and Elli could tell she was prepared to flee this uncomfortable moment.

Elli jumped in to rescue the situation, if possible. "What makes you think it's from Amy?" she asked.

He sighed. "She has been flirting with me. But I wish she wouldn't. She has been spending time with Ben, and Ben is one of my best friends. I don't like her playing up to him and then flirting with me."

He then held up the other card. "But this one really bewilders me. The card is signed by a Natalie Ann Taylor, and I have absolutely no idea who she is." Suddenly he smiled. "Hey, you two are my best friends as far as girls go. Why don't you help me find out who she is?"

Sarah's countenance brightened at his words, and the two girls agreed to join in the sleuthing to learn more about the mysterious girl. They spent much of the morning asking all their friends and fellow students. When the three met as agreed upon at lunch, none of them had anything to share. No one seemed to know anyone by that name.

As they tried to figure out how she could be unknown to everyone they had talked to, Sarah had an idea. "If no one knows her, that would mean she is new here."

"Then how do we find her?" Tyson asked.

They all thought for a time, and then Elli said, "I've got an idea. The secretaries would know her, especially if she is new."

They agreed that if she was new, they could ask the secretaries about her, and it wouldn't look stalkerish. So as soon as they finished lunch, they went to the office. But to their dismay, the secretaries had not heard of her, nor was she listed in the computer.

Through the afternoon, they continued to ask their teachers and other students. Still, the mystery remained unsolved by the time they met after school.

"This is beginning to freak me out," Tyson said. "I have some ghost girl who gave me a card."

He sighed. "Well, I better go before Taylor and Natalie leave me."

"Wait a minute," Elli said. "What did you just say?"

"I said I better get to the car before my sisters leave me, and I have to walk."

"Reverse their names," Elli said.

Tyson laughed. "You mean like Natalie and Taylor?"

Suddenly, Tyson and Sarah realized what Elli was saying. They rushed to Tyson's locker, pulled out the card, and read it. It said, "Have a great day, Natalie and Taylor."

"Well, in my defense," Tyson said, "the d doesn't have much of a stem and looks like an n."

When I arrived to pick Elli up from school, I saw Tyson and Sarah leaving. "Did your friends need a ride?" I asked.

Elli shook her head and smiled. "No. A mysterious girl made it so they could walk home together."

Cupcakes

Mary and Sally were neighbors and best friends. But sometimes, Mary shook her head at things Sally did. It was, as Mary described her friend, that Sally thought with her heart and not always with her head. Sally would get caught up in something and not think it through.

For example, one day, a radio D. J. talked about how someone had suggested that the signs for animal crossing should be moved away from the interstate since the interstate was a dangerous place for animals to cross. Sally heard this and didn't realize he was expressing it as humor. She was working on a letter to her congressional representative to get the signs moved when Mary came calling. Sally explained what she was doing, and it took Mary a good week to convince her that it was all in fun because animals can't read.

One day, Sally was busy trying to find a way to have braille put on the dashboard of cars so blind people could tell what speed they were going. Mary sighed at the thought of it. She wasn't even sure where Sally came up with that idea. She had probably heard someone lamenting they couldn't drive because of their failing eyesight, and she had thought it was because the person couldn't read the dashboard.

But even though Mary often shook her head at the things Sally came up with, she knew it was because Sally had such a big heart and wanted to help everyone. Though Sally often didn't think everything through, she was always first to take something to a sick neighbor or help a stray animal. Sally was always there for her own five children, but she didn't forget friends and neighbors either.

Mary couldn't count the number of times Sally had brought over cupcakes for one of Mary's children's birthdays. There was always an extra big bunch for Mary's birthday. Cupcakes were Sally's specialty, and she seemed to get a girlish delight in decorating them. And there were always lots of sprinkles.

That's why, when Mary was put in charge of the Parents' Baked Food Sale to raise money for new books at the grade school, she wasn't surprised to have Sally immediately volunteer to bring cupcakes. Mary gratefully accepted and then busied herself calling other mothers to bring different items. Soon, the list was all filled out, and the day was quickly approaching.

Mary didn't know why she grew concerned about Sally's food donation. Maybe it was because the episode of the football fundraising was still fresh on her mind. Sally didn't understand football and had come up with the idea that if they could raise enough money, they could buy more footballs so the two teams wouldn't have to fight over the same one.

Mary knew the cupcakes were critical to a good baked food sale, and as her concern grew, she decided to make some as a backup. She would just leave them in her car where they could be retrieved if they were needed.

The day of the fundraiser soon came. The mothers were asked to have their items there a half hour early so they could be set out for display. All were there on time except for Sally's. It was almost time to open the sale when she finally showed up. The cupcakes were beautiful, and Mary laughed at herself for doubting her friend.

"I'm so sorry these are late," Sally said, all out of breath. "Fluffers, our dog, licked all the frosting off of them, so I had to refrost them."

"Fluffers licked the frosting off of them?" Mary asked, trying not to gag.

Sally nodded. "And then he got sick as usual and threw up. You'd think he'd learn his lesson as often as he's done it."

"How often has he done it?" Mary asked.

"I think about every time I've made cupcakes," Sally said. "He just can't seem to control himself." Then Sally laughed. "It's a good thing I like to decorate cupcakes."

As Sally continued talking, it was all Mary could do not to gag as she thought about how many of Sally's cupcakes she had eaten. But somehow, when Sally finished, Mary still managed a weak smile and a thank you. Then, after Sally left, Mary dumped all the cupcakes into the garbage and retrieved the ones she made.

But she considered that she might never eat another cupcake again for as long as she lived.

Together

Ron and Edna got married very young. They didn't get much of a honeymoon because Ron owned nine milk cows, and someone had to be there to milk them. And once they got married, Edna joined Ron in the milking. She said it may not have been romantic, but they were together.

Then, not long after they were married, some of Ron's friends asked him if he wanted to go fishing with them. They planned to camp and fish all weekend. Ron could never really get away before. But then he thought about it and smiled.

"You know, I can go. I now have someone to milk the cows."

The problem was that Ron didn't consult with Edna about leaving her with all the chores. And when milking time came, and she realized she had all the tasks to do herself, she was not happy. When Ron came home Sunday night, she was waiting for him.

"What is the big idea of going off and leaving me to do the chores while you're fishing?" she demanded. "And you didn't even ask me."

Ron felt sheepish about it and tried to apologize.

"It's lucky you had the keys to the car, or maybe not lucky," Edna said. "Anyway, when I realized you had just taken off with your buddies, I decided I was just going to leave, and you could come home to be alone with your unmilked cows. But since the keys were gone, I decided to stay and milk them."

With some profuse apologies and planting some hedges of flowers that Edna loved, Ron was able to smooth things over. Then they had a good talk. Edna said she married him to spend time with him. It wasn't that she minded him going fishing with his friends now and then, but she said the decision should have been made together.

Ron realized he was wrong and agreed. And from then on, not only did they make their decisions together, but most of what they did was together. When the money from selling the milk didn't meet their needs as the family grew, they got a job together doing janitorial work. They would clean local churches to add to their income, and they always did it together.

Because they felt that work was also serving God, they always did the best job they could. People noticed and expressed their appreciation for Ron and Edna's work, which was always above what they were paid to do.

Ron and Edna also loved to work in their garden together. In the evenings, after they had finished their cleaning jobs, they could often be seen weeding, picking peas, or watering. They loved that time together.

Ron and Edna were my neighbors, and I can remember when he called and asked if I could use a pumpkin. Ron and Edna loved children, and I had a big family. He said he had one specially picked out for us.

I thanked him and told him my pumpkins hadn't fared too well. I had gotten busy during the summer, and the weeds in my garden were gaining the upper hand. I got in my van and drove over to Ron's house. When he showed me the pumpkin, I gasped.

"Ron, that's not a pumpkin," I said. "That's a round, orange pickup truck!"

He chuckled. "That's why you are the one who is going to move it."

It was probably close to three hundred pounds and more than three feet in diameter. Ron chuckled his contagious chuckle at my comment. Then I went back home to get my pickup. I knew I couldn't lift the pumpkin, so I got some 2X6 boards. I went back, and straining every muscle, I rolled it into my pickup.

My children decorated the pumpkin into the biggest jack-o'-lantern we have ever had. Some of the smaller children even climbed inside. They could completely fit in it if they curled up.

When it was all ready, Ron and Edna, always together, came to see the finished work.

(Continued)

Together Again

(Together part 2)

Ron and Edna were very young when they got married, but after a bit of a rough start, they did everything together. They especially liked to garden together. Many people in our small, rural community were recipients of produce from Ron and Edna's garden. I often received the biggest pumpkins I have ever seen outside of a National Geographic magazine picture.

Ron got so he really didn't like to do anything without Edna. If it was something just for the men in the community, he didn't want to go. But if something exciting or unusual was happening, he would rush home to get Edna, even if that meant he would miss part of it.

It could be when the girls and their fathers were having a mud pit pig catch for the daddy-daughter dates. It might be an old gravel road finally getting paved or ground being broken for a new home. If it was something he was interested in, he wanted to share it with Edna.

But then Edna got really sick. Ron never left her side, other than to get things she needed. Even then, he might ask a neighbor to pick up a prescription or grab some groceries so he could stay by her side. With Ron's tender care, Edna pulled through.

Then came the year that Ron and Edna didn't plant a garden. Even as they grew old and struggled to maintain the garden, they had always had one. So, when no garden was planted, I knew their health must be declining. The good people of the community returned the favor they had received over the years and shared their garden harvest with Ron and Edna.

A few more years went on, and then, in a very short time, Ron's health plummeted. He suddenly didn't have the strength to take care of himself. Ron was a big man, and Edna was a small woman. She could not manage alone, but she didn't want Ron to be in an assisted living home or anyplace away from her.

With Edna's permission, the men of the community organized to help. I took two mornings and one evening each week. I would go in the morning and help get Ron up, to the bathroom, or anything else he needed, and then to his chair. At night, I would reverse the process. Ron had always been independent, and it was hard for him to accept the help, but he was grateful to stay with Edna.

When I would knock on the door, their little dog, Dude, would make a fuss trying to protect them.

Ron or Edna would yell, "Dude, knock it off. He's okay."

Dude would then let me come in. After a while, Dude got used to me and greeted me at the door. He seemed happy to see me because, once Ron settled into his chair, Dude could curl up in his lap. When I finished helping Ron, I often sat down to visit, and his positive spirit helped me.

Sometimes he told me stories about him and Edna. He knew his time was growing short, so other times he asked me to share my feelings about what happens after death.

And then one morning, just as I was leaving to help Ron, I got word from Edna that he was gone.

Ron's loss was hard on Edna, and the good people from the community often stopped to visit. One time when I stopped in, Edna expressed how much she missed him. Then she said, "Tell me again what you shared with Ron."

I nodded. "I believe that when we die, we will be with those we love. The Savior told us to love one another, and love transcends the greatest challenges of all, even death. If we are not with those we love in heaven, it wouldn't be heaven. It would actually feel like a punishment for loving others as we have been told. God would never punish us for doing what he asked. You and Ron will be together again."

Edna smiled. "I believe that, too. I just like hearing you say it."

Recently, Edna left us to join Ron. I imagine some big, exciting event was happening in heaven, and Ron didn't want Edna to miss it, so he came to get her. That's what he always used to do when he was here.

Glow in the Dark

When I was scoutmaster, we had our meetings on Tuesday nights. The girls of the same age had activities at the same time. On one Tuesday a month, the boys and girls met together and had an activity. The boys and girls would trade off who was in charge, and this time it was the girls' turn.

"Tell your boys that they need to each wear a white T-shirt this Tuesday," Kay, the girls' leader, said.

"What are we doing?" I asked.

"We want to keep that a secret until you get there," she replied.

Keeping it a secret usually meant it was an activity the girls were dying to do, and the boys would rather not. But I passed the word along. The boys wanted to know what we were doing, but I couldn't tell them.

"They did say there would be good treats, though," I replied.

"It better not be karaoke singing again," Gordy replied. "That was just too weird."

"Only because you can't sing," Mort replied.

"Yeah, well, when you got up there, I thought somebody's calf must have gotten stuck in the fence and was bawling for its mother," Gordy replied.

"Okay, okay," I said. "I'm sure it will be fun. So, wear your white T-shirt and come prepared to have a good time."

When Tuesday came, we had a good turnout, partly because everyone was curious about what we were doing. When we got into the church activity hall, Kay announced the activity.

"Tonight, we are going to play blacklight volleyball," she said.

She flipped off the lights and turned on the blacklight. Suddenly, everyone looked like a floating T-shirt. I could see very little else. Some of the young people had white tennis shoes, and they stood out, too. Those people looked like running feet below a floating shirt.

"So, where's the ball?" Gordy called out in the darkness.

"I have it," Kay said. She tossed it up. "See it."

But we didn't see it, so Kay turned the lights back on. "I thought for sure it would glow in the blacklight," Kay said.

The volleyball was a grayish-white color. But whether it was the color or the material it was made of, it did not reflect the black light. Kay was desperate to salvage the activity. She looked around, trying to think of what to do, then she apparently hit on a plan.

Gordy was her son, and she said to him, "Gordy, give me your shirt. You can go shirtless to play tonight."

"That will be a disgusting sight," Mort said.

"It will be dark," Kay replied, not catching the sarcasm.

Kay took the ball and wrapped it in Gordy's shirt. She then wrapped a bunch of clear tape around it to ensure it stayed. The teams were formed with half the boys and half the girls on each team. The lights were shut off, and the game began. It was kind of fun to see the glowing ball moving back and forth and trying to hit it without running into a floating T-shirt. Gordy was on the other team, and his white shoes were all I could see of him.

As the game progressed, the shirt began unraveling from the ball. Mort was near the net, and the ball was coming straight toward him when the shirt fell off the ball completely. But he had already determined its trajectory. He jumped and made a perfect hit into what he thought was an open space on the other side of the net.

He hadn't seen Gordy's shoes there, and Gordy couldn't see the invisible ball coming. Suddenly, there was a loud smack and an even louder thud. The lights were quickly turned on, and Gordy, with a puffy black eye beginning to show, was lying dazed on the floor.

"I'm sorry," Mort said. "I couldn't see you."

The game was called, and everyone moved to the kitchen for ice-cream sandwiches.

Kay was frustrated that she couldn't find an icepack for her son. I handed her my ice cream sandwich.

"Try this," I said. "The truly edible icepack."

Living the Dream

I think we have all had those dreams, the ones where we aren't prepared for something important. Back in my high school and college days, when I was in athletics, I had them a lot. I would dream we went to an away football game, and when we got there, I realized I had forgotten my pads, helmet, and everything.

I would usually have my jersey. We always wore that to school the day of the game to remind everyone to come cheer for us. But all of the essential stuff was missing.

The same would be true with wrestling. I would dream I was at a big tournament and had forgotten my wrestling clothes. I was forced to wrestle in my regular clothes, which were not flexible and were hard to move in. Likewise, during track season, I would dream all I had were my big work boots and clothes that were heavy enough I felt like I was dressed in knightly armor.

The strange thing about these dreams was that no one else noticed. In football, the coach would put me into play as if nothing was amiss. I would line up across from the opposing linemen with all their gear, helmets, and pads. I would think to myself in the dream, "This isn't going to end well." But then, just as the ball was hiked, and we surged forward toward one another, I woke up. I think it was my brain's way of saving me from destruction.

Though the dreams are less frequent now than when I was participating in sports, they still come occasionally. But probably the type of dream that occurred the most, and still does, has to do with college classes.

I was in a meeting at the university where I work, and the speaker was an engineer. He talked of just such a dream. He said he was working through his degree, and it was getting toward the end of his last semester, when he realized he had totally forgotten about a class. By the grins on people's faces, it was easy to see he was not alone in this type of dream. I know I have had them many times.

The speaker continued on to say that in his dream, it was a class outside his major, one that he had to pass to graduate, but also one he knew nothing about. He rushed to prepare for the final coming up, hoping it would allow him to pass. He went to everyone he knew that was in the class, and they didn't seem to know anything. When I have dreamed these types of dreams, the other students had also forgotten they had the class, but they didn't seem to care. I was the only one who was concerned.

He said in his dream, try as he might, he couldn't find out anything. My dreams were always similar. The professor couldn't be found, the book was in a language I didn't understand, and all the tutors were on vacation. I dreamed that in utter desperation, I decided to attempt the final. Maybe it would be multiple choice or something, and I could at least guess.

I would sit down to take the test, and my heart would be pounding. When word came to turn the test over and start, to my dismay, I found the test was also in a foreign language and all answers were essay questions. That would be when my brain would wake me, saving me from total failure.

As the speaker shared his similar dreams, I looked around the hall, and just about everyone was smiling. The experience, though perhaps somewhat different for each of us, was something we all related to. But then, as he finished, he looked out over all those college students and grinned.

"And all of you young people here today are just living the dream."

The Best Decision

Back in the late eighties and early nineties, when the internet was new, I was the director of internet services at a small religious college. Even email was new, and one semester we had an interesting dilemma arise.

One young man, I'll call John, caused problems. It was a big thing back then to post something and then add that a person should pass it on to a certain number of friends for good luck. The idea was to push a message as wide as possible, a precursor to something going viral today.

We had already caught John multiple times hacking into different computer systems. Each time I tracked the attacks back to his computer, I turned his name in to the student discipline office. Every time I did, they only told him to stop, then let it go. I couldn't get them to understand the severity of what he was doing. They ignored my suggestion to expel him so he would not have access to our systems.

Then one day, I got a call from the college president's secretary. "Daris, have you seen the crass email that was sent out by one of our students?" I told her I hadn't, so she said she would forward it to me. "After you read it, you will need to hurry to an emergency meeting that starts in fifteen minutes in the conference room in the President's Suite. The president wants you and all the vice-presidents to discuss it with him."

I printed the email and read it as I hurried to the meeting. It was a very disgusting joke that was extremely degrading to women. At the bottom, it included two things. The first was the admonition to pass it on to five friends for good luck. The second was a banner making it look like the email was official and approved by the college. John was the sender.

At the meeting, the president told us that the CEO of a big company had called and was very upset. He was one of our alumni, and his secretary had gotten a copy of the email. She had brought it to him and disgustedly asked if the college he graduated from sanctioned that was the kind of stuff. The CEO, a college donor, was mortified and wanted an explanation.

Our college president had done his best to calm the man down, and he assured him that it was not sent with the college's permission. When the college president finished telling the story, he asked, "What should we do about this?"

A unanimous, loud consensus quickly grew among the vice presidents that John should be required to send out a retraction as a condition for him to stay at the school. I sat quietly, feeling very much out of place with these men. Finally, the president noticed I had said nothing, and turned to me.

"Daris, what do you think?"

"Frankly," I said, "I think that trying to send out a retraction is about the worst thing you could do."

The vice presidents seemed stunned I would speak so boldly and forcefully against what they had said. The president seemed surprised, but asked, "What do you propose?"

"I once heard a story of a man who was libeled by someone in the newspaper. In great anger, he went to the editor and asked him what he should do to make sure people knew it was false. The editor said the best thing to do was nothing. He said that half the people don't take the paper. Half of those who do won't read it. Half who read it won't see that column. Half of those that see that column won't read it. Half that read it won't understand it. And half that understand won't believe it. He then said that the few that believe it are the ones who are of little consequence."

I then faced all the men in that room and said, "If a retraction is sent out, those who haven't read the email will decide to read it to find out what the fuss is about. The best thing we can do is remove the student from our campus so we have no repeats, and allow the memory of the email to die away."

Everyone seemed to ponder that, then the president called for a vote. It was unanimous to do as I suggested. And though there was another time the story came back to cause me grief, it mostly faded away.

It is true that sometimes the best thing to do is nothing.

Internet Ethics

When the president's council at the university wanted to force a student to send out a retraction on a nasty joke he emailed, I advised against it, suggesting it would be better to do nothing. That way it would die away faster. And even though the email made it look like the joke was college-approved, that ended up being a good decision.

For the most part, it faded away quickly. But a couple of weeks after the email was sent, our network servers came under a heavy DDoS (Distributed Denial of Service) attack. Our systems were flooded with so much traffic that the normal functions were brought to a standstill. For all intents and purposes, to our internet users, it looked as if our servers were down.

When I got to work and realized what was happening, I immediately shut down the ports where the traffic was coming in. I determined the IP addresses of the attack and blocked them at the gateways. Gradually, I was able to bring the systems back up. Meanwhile, I received a lot of angry phone calls and emails from users across campus.

"Don't you know that we're getting so we rely on these systems?" one caller said. "I had material I needed for class on the internet. You can't just start taking them down."

No amount of explanation could convince them it wasn't my fault. As the systems came back and the angry calls and emails abated, I found our email systems overloaded with junk email. I worked to clear that out, returning the systems' efficiency. It took me until well into the morning hours to get everything back to normal. By the time I got home, I was tired, hungry, and upset. My children were asleep, and I didn't get my usual evening time with my family.

The next day, I traced out where the traffic had come from. Often in a DDoS attack, the person instigating it will put viruses on unsuspecting user machines, making it so the traffic comes from all over, and the origin of the instigator is almost impossible to detect. But in this case, everything had come from the computers of one organization.

I must admit that in my anger I was tempted to create havoc on their machines. I had the skills to do it. But then I thought about the ethics I taught my students in my networking class. Because I taught them powerful skills they could use for hacking and other malicious endeavors, I spent an entire week talking about ethics. I told them:

1) Never do something illegal.

2) Just because something is legal doesn't make it right. Never do something that is wrong.

3) Remember that just because you can doesn't mean you should.

4) Never do something on the internet in an angry response, but take time to calm down.

5) Don't do it if it hurts someone.

6) Anything you do on the internet becomes a permanent record of you and will usually come back to haunt you if it is bad.

I took my own advice and spent a couple of days calming down. Then I contacted the administrator of the network where the attack came from. I told him I had traced the attack back to their computers, and I wanted to know what was happening.

I got a terse reply from him. He did the attack because he was angry. His ten-year-old daughter had gotten the nasty joke in her email, making her cry.

I suppose I could have reported the incident to the police, but instead, I chose to apologize. I told him the email did not represent who we were, was not sanctioned by the university, and the student had been expelled. I also told him I understood how he felt. I had daughters of my own, and because of what he did, I had to work most of the night, and I didn't get to see them that day. He responded with an apology of his own, and we opened a dialogue that resulted in a wonderful friendship between us.

As I look at some of the offensive postings I see on the internet, I wish more people would consider internet ethics. I often wonder if those who post them remember that at the other end is a person with feelings much like themselves.

Pranks and April Fools

My computer science class was comprised of forty-four boys and one girl. That was typical back then. If I even had one girl, I felt lucky. A girl in the class always added a dimension that I can't explain. But sometimes, when there were only one or two girls, they would feel out of place and drop my class.

But Tasha was different. It was like she was one of the boys. In fact, she was almost more so. I know that sounds strange, so I will explain.

In most of my classes, the boys were the ones that played the pranks. But in that particular class, it was always Tasha. I think that maybe, being a girl in what was then a male-dominated discipline, it was her way of asserting herself.

She had probably played a prank on every boy in the class. Though I saw some in person, there were others done outside of class that I only heard about secondhand. The pranks were all sorts of things. I'll share a couple of examples.

David had forgotten to log off the computer he was using when he was sitting by Tasha. I had a little batch program that I installed into students' accounts when I saw that occur. It produced a warning the next time they logged in. Tasha had been on the receiving end of that at least once, having herself forgotten to log out. She took the little file and manipulated it.

When David left his computer logged in and went home, she slid over to the chair he had been in and copied the file to his account. The next time he logged in, the screen showed an oversize image with a skull and crossbones. It said, "Since you didn't log out, all of your files have been deleted to protect your information."

You can imagine the panic that caused when David saw it, thinking all of his files and critical work for class were destroyed. They, of course, were there, but it took him a moment to get to them. He was not the only one she did this to. She might have had different variations for each person, but she caused near heart attacks in multiple members of our class.

For Jack, she played a different prank. He left his computer briefly to go to the restroom after he finished his program for the week. She slid into his chair and added a line of code inside the main loop. It was a program the students had to demonstrate in class. When Jack brought it up the next day, it flashed on the screen, "Jack, I'm not sure I believe that!" every time he entered something.

As the semester was ending, the boys asked me about doing a prank in return. I told them that it was between them and Tasha, and I was staying out of it. But that changed one morning.

As I walked into the building I work in, I saw a picture on the door. I glanced at it quickly and saw that it said the person needed a date to the spring formal. Students often posted fliers like that, so I ignored it and continued on. But as I got halfway up to my office, something in my mind triggered recognition. I hurried back downstairs to the door and inspected the picture. It was one of me in my wrestling uniform taken from the yearbook when I was in college. It had a sad story about supposed challenges in my life and that I could really use a nice date with a good young lady. The number it said to call to offer to go out with me was my office phone.

At first, I wondered who would have done such a thing, but then, like a lightning bolt, I knew it had to be Tasha. I also knew she never did anything small, and I realized she wouldn't just put it on the door where I would see it. I hurried to all the buildings on campus and found the picture on every entrance. It took me well over an hour to retrieve all I could find. I hoped I had averted any embarrassing phone calls, but when I got back to my office, my phone was already ringing off the hook. I spent a good part of the day explaining to well-meaning young ladies that I really wasn't desperate for a date.

That was when I decided that perhaps the young men were right. We should return the joke favor and play one on Tasha, especially since April Fools was only days away.

(Continued)

Pranks and April Fools

(Part 2)

Tasha, the only girl in my computer science class, had played a joke on every boy in the class. They wanted my help to get her back, but I told them I was staying out of it. That is, I was until she played one on me. Then I finally agreed to join them. We had a meeting to make our plan.

"What would embarrass Tasha the most?" I asked. "What does she dislike?"

"Guys," David responded to the second question. "I think she really despises us."

"Yeah," Samuel said. "I think she has an issue with having anyone think she could ever like a boy."

"Well, maybe that's it, then," Steven said. "We find a way to make it look like she's head over heels for some man. That would embarrass her the most."

"But she would likely kill the guy we used," David said.

"So let's use a fictitious one," Steven replied.

"And let's have it ready to do on April Fool's," Samuel added.

From that point, I mostly just listened to their plan. The real reason they wanted me to be involved was so I would go along with anything they wanted to plan in the classroom. I told them it could embarrass Tasha as she had done to so many of them, but I didn't want her hurt.

Finally, the plan was coming together. The boys found a picture of Tasha in the previous year's yearbook. They then searched magazines at the library or anything else they had. (This was before internet days.) They all brought the best one they could find. They settled on one that one of them had from a relative getting married. They used software to superimpose Tasha's face in place of the bride. They also changed the face of the groom so he was very unpleasant looking. They didn't want him to be recognizable at all. Then they dolled up the background to make the wedding look foolishly lavish.

Next, they all pooled their money and purchased a big ad in the school newspaper. Below the picture were the words, "Congratulations on your recent marriage from all of your friends in computer science."

There were enough of them that for a dollar each, they were able to take out a half-page ad. I couldn't wait to see it. And right on schedule, on April Fool's, the ad came out. When I came in the morning, I hurried and grabbed the newspaper from the free bin just inside the door as I entered the building. On page three, just after flipping open the paper, the picture was as big as life. It was amazingly good, or amazingly bad, however you want to think about it. I wondered what Tasha's reaction would be.

Class was at ten, and all the young men were there early, as was I. When Tasha walked in, she stopped, and scanned the room with a glare. Now was my part.

I could barely keep a straight face as I spoke. "Tasha, I saw the paper today. I'm amazed. I didn't even know you were dating anyone. I'd like to offer my congratulations."

Tasha's scowl deepened. "It is not true, and somebody is going to die today."

Still holding back my smile, I shrugged. "Well, if you aren't really married, then what is this?"

One boy ran and threw open the door and signaled to others in the hall. The room filled with friends of Tasha's from all over campus that the boys had invited. They were followed by a mariachi band. The band started playing love songs for Tasha. The boys began clapping along to the songs, and everyone joined in; everyone but Tasha. I'm not sure if the look on Tasha's face was one of embarrassment or a simple desire to kill someone.

It was a joyous celebration, and the boys had even purchased a wedding cake. It went on for about half the class time before I shooed everyone out so I could get some teaching in. When they left, I said, "We missed the celebration, Tasha, so we wanted to give you one of our own."

She smiled good-naturedly. "Yeah. Well, I still think someone is going to die for this."

(Continued)

Pranks and April Fools

(Final)

Tasha, the only girl in my computer class, had played a prank on every boy. After she also played one on me, we organized an April Fool's joke on her, making it look like she was married.

I knew she was embarrassed and a bit mad, so l was somewhat surprised when she came to my office the next day.

"You know, Professor Howard," she said, "I was so embarrassed and mad at all of you yesterday that I was about ready to hospitalize someone. But it got me thinking about the reasons I play pranks on the guys."

"And why is that?" I asked.

"I think it is two reasons," she replied. "I love science, especially computer science. But in high school, my teachers kept telling me I couldn't do those things because I am a girl. I want men to feel I can be just as good as they are and respect my ability. But I realized maybe I was trying to get their attention, too. I have never had a date, ever. Almost everyone in computer science is male, and maybe I hoped they might see that I'm not."

"So, you want to show you are as good as a man but still be a woman?"

She pondered that for a minute, then slowly nodded. "I suppose that's it. I just wish I could at least go to the spring formal this week."

"Well, Tasha, it isn't because you aren't pretty, because you are. I think it's just the young men get thinking of you as one of them, and asking you out seems strange."

We had a nice long talk before she headed back to the computer lab to do her assignments. But then I had another interesting visit. Albert Einstein said that a coincidence is nothing but God doing his work anonymously. I totally believe that, and about a half hour after Tasha left my office, Jack came.

"Professor Howard, would you know any girl that might like to go on a date?" he asked. "I am getting ready to graduate, and I haven't even been on a single date. I just don't know any girls because there aren't any in computer science."

I thought, "Do I have the girl for you," but instead, I simply said, "What about Tasha?"

Jack looked stunned. "Oh, my heavens, Tasha is a girl, isn't she?" Then his face showed his embarrassment as he stammered on. "I mean, of course she is. I just never thought of her as a dating kind of girl."

I smiled. "I just happen to know that Tasha would love to have someone ask her to the spring formal."

"But do you think she would go out with someone like me?" he asked. "There are so many better guys."

"Jack, Tasha sits by you, and I don't think that is just by chance. I think she likes you."

"But she plays more pranks on me than anyone."

"I think that is for the same reason," I replied. Jack seemed stunned by all of this. Then I said, "But you better ask her soon, since the formal is tomorrow, and someone else might ask her."

A steely look of determination came into Jack's eyes. "I'll go ask her right now."

All weekend I wondered how it went, but on Monday, in class, with the way Jack and Tasha smiled at each other, I knew they had had a good time together. And at graduation, they were holding hands as they walked through the line.

We were only a two-year junior college then, and I learned from them that they planned to go to the same four-year university so they could continue dating. I seldom hear from my students how things turn out as they go on with their lives, but about a year later, I received a wedding announcement from Jack and Tasha. They looked beautiful together.

I was sure Jack would always support Tasha in her love of science, but I also knew that if their marriage ever got mundane, or Jack didn't pay enough attention to her, Tasha wasn't above playing a prank on him to get his attention.

Helping a Neighbor, or Not

Seth was busy working on his four-wheeler for a trip into the mountains the next day with a group of mid-teen boys. That was when his neighbor showed up.

"Good morning, Seth," the neighbor said.

Seth, holding a couple of bolts in his mouth, nodded a greeting.

"Seth," the neighbor continued, "could you do me a favor and drop my cows a bale of hay in their feeder tomorrow morning? It won't be hard. You just need to fire up the old farmhand tractor, and I have already loaded a bale of hay on it. Just drive it into the pasture and dump the bale in the feeder."

Seth was leery of accepting the task. The neighbor didn't have the best equipment, and when Seth had worked for him before, something had always gone wrong. Maybe the tractor wouldn't start or something. He didn't want to miss meeting up with his friends and get left behind for the four-wheeling trip.

The neighbor must have sensed Seth's concern. He told of his desire to get away for a family gathering and ended by saying, "The old tractor runs like a top."

Seth slowly nodded. He knew how hard it was to get away when there were animals to feed. Besides, what could go wrong with just dumping a single bale into a feeder? The neighbor thanked him and headed on his way.

The next morning, Seth went to do the feeding early to have plenty of time before meeting the other guys. At the neighbor's house, everything was just as described. The tractor was sitting by the gate with the one-ton bale loaded on the forks.

Seth opened the gate, fired up the tractor, and drove it toward the feeder. The feeder was a fair distance across the pasture. It sat about thirty yards from where the pasture dropped toward the river. Seth gunned the tractor to full speed to hurry and get the job done.

Seth hit the clutch and gently pushed on the brakes as he approached the feeder. The clutch disengaged the engine from pushing the tractor forward, but the brakes didn't seem to slow the tractor at all. He pushed the brake pedal farther and farther until it was against the floor, but he wasn't seeing much, if any, effect. He was still heading at a good clip toward the feeder.

Realizing he was going to run over the feeder, he veered off. The hill was coming up fast, so he tried to turn the tractor along the hill rim, but a deep canal blocked his path. The tractor had only slowed a little before it went over the edge of the hill.

On the downward slope, the tractor picked up speed. Seth pumped the brakes, but there was still no effect. He tried to use the engine to slow the tractor. He throttled down and let off the clutch. The tractor sputtered and smoked and slowed a bit, but the clutch started to slip.

At the bottom of the hill was a deep swamp. Seth knew if he went into it, the tractor would sink nearly out of sight. He looked desperately for a way out of his predicament. That was when he saw the old tree stump. He turned the tractor toward it and lowered the bucket.

The cows had heard the tractor and were coming up the hill to eat. Seth yelled at them to get out of the way. Most of them did. But as cows always seem to do, one on the right side of the tractor decided she had to dash across to the left. There was nothing Seth could do. The tractor hit her, rolling her most of the way to the swamp. But as he hoped, the tractor also hit the stump and came to an instant stop.

Seth took some deep breaths, put the tractor in reverse, and backed up the hill. He carefully loaded the hay in the feeder, then put the tractor back in the hay yard. Finally, he went to check on the injured cow. But as he came close, she limped away on three legs at a dead run, looking like a drunken peg-legged sailor in a life-and-death race. Seth couldn't get close enough to check on her no matter how he tried. He decided if she could run like that, she would live, and he left to meet his friends.

A few days later, the neighbor stopped by to thank Seth for his work. "You know, it seems like every time I leave, one of the animals has trouble. Old number fifteen is so lame she can hardly walk. It appears she slipped and rolled down the hill."

Seth just left it at that.

A Matter of Independence

Arthur was both independent and stubborn. As he got older, it was hard for him to accept help. His good neighbors kept asking him what they could do for him, but he always told them he was managing everything okay. The youth in the community would mow his lawn and rake his leaves in the fall, and it about killed him. He felt he could do it himself. So, if the grass barely had any growth or even a few leaves were on the ground, he was out there working to get matters taken care of before someone showed up and did it for him.

Arthur needed surgery, and as word got out about it, everyone wanted to help even more. People would visit with him at church or stop by if they saw him out in his yard. It became so frequent he would hurry into the house if he saw a car coming, only to go back out when the coast was clear.

One day, he saw a group of people walking down the road, and he quickly ducked into the house to avoid them. But as they got closer, he realized it was just the older women in the community out on their evening walk. He watched them from his big picture window.

When they got to the big tree by his driveway, the branches hung so low over the road that the women had to go around them. He was embarrassed that he had let it get that way. He had noticed the growth earlier and planned to do something about it, but he never got it done. A little later, when someone stopped to see if they could help him, he almost mentioned the tree. But then he considered that he could do it after his surgery.

The next day he went into the hospital and had his surgery. It wasn't supposed to be any big deal, and he thought he'd be out in a day—two at most. But as old as he was, he was there most of two weeks. The pain, recovery, and exhaustion took a toll on him, and he didn't eat well. The doctor expressed concern about the amount of weight Arthur lost. But eventually, Arthur was released, and his wife drove him home.

Arthur still had some healing to do, but after a few more days, the doctor told Arthur he could get back to his activities if he worked slowly, carefully, didn't overexert himself, and ate better so his weight would come back to a normal level. That was a joyful day for Arthur. They had barely returned from the doctor appointment when Arthur was trying to decide what he would do first.

That was when he saw the ladies' group coming down the road. He thought of the tree and grabbed the loppers.

"Remember the doctor's orders," his wife reminded him. "Nothing too strenuous."

"I'll just cut off some of the smaller tree branches to make it so people can walk under it," he said on his way out the door.

Arthur could see the ladies approaching and hurried to get enough cut so they wouldn't have to skirt the tree branches. If he was honest, he had to admit that he wanted them to see that he was back to work, and his surgery wasn't holding him down.

By the time he got to the tree, the ladies were only about thirty yards away. He gallantly reached the loppers up to cut the most offending branch to clear the path for the women. But that was when an issue he hadn't counted on came into play. Though he had his belt cinched up to the tightest notch, it wasn't sufficient for the amount of weight he had lost. Just as the ladies reached the tree, and just as Arthur did his first snip, his pants fell to his ankles.

At that point, Arthur debated what to do. He considered that there was no way to undo what had just happened, so he just continued to snip branches until the ladies had passed, acting like it was all a normal thing. He hoped that not making a big deal of it would help everyone forget about it sooner.

But when an older widow stopped by one day to visit with his wife, Arthur heard them talking, and he realized it might be hard to live down what had happened.

Both women laughed when the woman said, "Your husband sure knows how to put on a good show."

Arthur decided that maybe he shouldn't be too proud to admit he could use some help now and then.

It's More Than the Building

It is a tough time to be building a house. I should know; I've been trying to do just that since February 2021. I have added on to my current house twice. The first time I worked with a contractor. The second time I was the contractor. I learned how to line up materials so everything came at the right time and there was no break in the work. I did all the labor myself and learned a lot as I went.

This time, I am building a house from the ground up. Actually, I'm not yet building my house. We don't have money for that. We need to sell our current house first. But we can't sell it until we have a place to move everything, and we can't move everything until we have a place to put it, so we are building a shop.

When I was ready to start, I called all the material suppliers to see how far out they were on delivery. The ICF (insulated concrete forms) supplier told me that once I ordered, the blocks would be ready in four days. The trusses were six weeks out, so I ordered them first. I got everything lined up, then ordered the ICF blocks.

"They are now out four weeks," the block manufacturer said.

My heart sank. "Four weeks? You said it would be four days!"

"That was before we got deep into Covid," she answered.

I got them ordered, knowing everything was going to be thrown off schedule. It ended up being six weeks before they came, and they were the wrong ones. I sold them and turned around and reordered the right ones.

"It's now ten weeks," the lady told me.

I could see my whole summer flying away. The blocks weren't ten weeks in coming; they were seventeen weeks. I got them in December. We bought some blocks left over from other jobs and were able to get the walls high enough to pour the floor just before Thanksgiving. Then the blocks came, and I worked through the winter in freezing, sub-zero weather, building and getting ready to pour the walls the first of March. On one frigid day, as the wind blew icy snow particles into my skin, I was feeling sorry for myself when I thought of a home I visited in Peru.

I was there with some university colleagues on an academic trip. When we took time off from discovery to visit the local markets, I would often leave my colleagues and spend time seeing how the normal Peruvians lived. On one such excursion in a rural town, I came across a man sitting in front of his house. There was a sign that said, "See beautiful most town home. One dollar or one sol."

Though the English wasn't clear, through my limited Spanish and his equally limited English, I learned the man felt he had the most beautiful home in the town. He claimed he was the richest man there.

I handed him a sol, and he proudly led me into his home. The walls were not thatched reeds like most of the houses, but were handmade mud brick. "Best mud available, made self," he said. It also had a tin roof, made with tin that looked like he had salvaged it from the town dump where I live. The floor was dirt, and there was no electricity. The lighting all came from windows and candles. There was only one room that served as the kitchen, living room, and bedroom for all seven people who lived there.

I met his family—his wife, three daughters, a son, and his mother. They were all happy to be together, and the love that emanated from them for each other was evident.

On that day that I felt sorry for myself freezing and building on our new property, I thought of this man. He really was the richest man, not for what he owned, but for the love and happiness of his family. It made me feel a little warmer just thinking that a home is much more than the building.

It is more about the people who live, love, and share their lives there.

Learning to Eat Anything

Our daughter called in complete frustration. "Dad, Mom, how in the world am I supposed to get my children to eat their dinner? I've tried everything to get them to try new things and eat things they aren't fond of, but nothing works. What did you do when we were growing up?"

I thought about when I was young. I had five brothers, most of them older than me. We worked hard hauling hay, changing pipe, and all sorts of farm labor. When we came in for lunch, we were starving. Though my mom would have huge bowls full of potatoes, plates of steak and roast, and enormous pitchers of gravy, it didn't take long for everything to disappear. If we didn't get in and eat, we got nothing.

I don't remember ever being fussy about food. My parents insisted we try new dishes. "If you eat it, you'll learn to like it," was my mother's motto.

"What do you do if they don't eat it?" my wife, Donna, asked our daughter.

"We finally give in and let them eat a sandwich or something," she said. "We can't stand making them go to bed hungry."

"You're not making them go to bed hungry," Donna replied. "They're choosing to go to bed hungry."

"That's right," I added. "I think that one of the best things a parent can do for a child is to let them face the consequences of their decisions. In life, when someone chooses not to do something because they don't like it, there is not always going to be someone there to rescue them from getting fired or facing the consequences of their actions."

"We also used desserts as an incentive," Donna said. "If you didn't eat what was for dinner, you didn't get dessert."

I had to smile at this one. When this daughter was young, she didn't like green beans. When she was two years old, she used to slip them over the edge of the high chair tray to the floor when we weren't looking. More than once, she had been praised for eating her meal, and been rewarded with dessert, only to find a small pile of beans under her chair.

We told her that was not allowed. So, one day, Donna and I were visiting as we ate. I had my arm resting against our daughter's high chair. She could be very territorial, and even at two, she would usually push my arm away. But on this particular day, she just kept playing with my sleeve. When it came time for dessert, her tray was empty, and there was nothing on the floor. She received her praise and dessert. But when I stood up to take my plate to the sink, a whole pile of green beans slid out of my sleeve.

Now, with children of her own, she decided to try the things we suggested. Later, she called to tell us most of what we had told her worked. She said cutting out the snacks when the children refused to eat their meals took care of most of it. But her oldest daughter was very stubborn and sometimes was willing to be hungry if it was something she didn't want to eat.

The dessert had taken care of most of that issue. Even if the children didn't like something, they might eat it to get the dessert.

"But there is one thing that happens now," our daughter said. "My oldest wants to know what the desserts are before she decides whether or not she will eat the meals. But I have even figured out what to do for that."

"What is that?" I asked.

"I simply make her favorite desserts for the same meals I cook something she doesn't like."

I smiled. It's fun seeing our children deal with things we had to face with them.

A Matter of Honesty

One evening, my daughter, Celese, heard a noise outside her house. She flipped on the outside lights, and she and her husband went to investigate. What they found made Celese's heart sink. The tires on their pickup were slashed. Celese's sister was visiting them for the evening, and the worn-out tires on her old car were slashed, too. The pickup tires made Celese mad, but her sister's bald tires made her angrier. Her younger sister was struggling to buy a new, small house and make ends meet, and she couldn't afford new tires.

As Celese thought about it, she was sure she knew who had done it. She ran a small bookkeeping business. Most of her clients were small, but she had gotten a new, much larger one. She was learning that those she worked for that had the most money were the ones who tried to undercut her pay, if they paid at all. Unfortunately, the owner of this company was also asking her to do some unscrupulous things. She refused and decided they needed to part ways. He wasn't subtle about making some threats.

She thought some of her neighbors might have video cameras, and maybe she could collect some evidence. But then she considered that perhaps it would be easier to play her hand against his conscience and fear of legal action. She sent him a simple text that said, "That was a stupid thing to do with all the cameras we have in the neighborhood."

His reply was immediate and panicked. "I'm sorry. You're right; that was a stupid thing to do. Please don't call the police. It would ruin my family and my business. I will pay to make it right."

Neither the truck nor the car could be driven, so Celese had someone come remove the tires. She got new ones that were the best she could find. She sent the man the bill for all of it. When he got it, he answered in an obviously surprised text.

"You are only charging me $1400 for the two sets of tires and

$500 for labor? You're not going to charge me like $20,000 to not go to the police."

Celese responded with a text of her own. "What I charged was what it cost us. If I charged you more, it would be more like blackmail, which is wrong. If a person is dishonest with others, he or she can expect to get dishonesty in return."

Not too long passed before the man called. "I thought a lot about what you said. Almost everyone I have dealt with has tried to cheat me, so I felt it was okay for me to cheat others in return. I realize I was simply compounding the problem and justifying their actions. I'm sorry for what I did but grateful for what you taught me. I plan to change my business to one built on trust. If you ever forgive me for what I've done, I'd love to have you back as a bookkeeper, and I would never ask you to do something dishonest again."

Celese said she'd think about it. The man said even though she wasn't asking for more, he was going to send extra as a thank you, and she need not feel guilty about accepting it.

When Celese got the check, she was surprised to find it was more than double what she had billed him for. Along with it came a nice note, again expressing his gratitude.

"What are you going to do with the extra money?" her husband asked.

Celese grinned. "Well, part of it is going into a security system to help keep the honest people honest."

Careful of Wording

My three-year-old daughter brought me her toy. "Daddy, you fix for me?" It was a little wooden duck and just needed a little glue. I got some glue, put it on the broken joint, and pushed the two pieces together. I must have put on too much glue because some dripped down my hand. My little daughter stood close by, watching me. I wanted to hold it steady while the glue was setting, so I turned to her.

"Sweetheart, could you go ask Mommy for a damp cloth for me?"

"A what?" she asked.

"A damp cloth."

She hurried off to her mother, who was in the kitchen. It wasn't long before I heard my wife exclaim in dismay. "Your father asked you to get what?"

Suddenly, I realized how what I said might come out of the mouth of a three-year-old.

"I said damp-p-p-p-p cloth!" I called out. "There was a p on the end of that."

I've learned that a person must be careful what they say to a child. Even if the child says it right, it often sounds different coming from them.

A good example of this was the first time we took our youngest children to the ocean. Our older ones had been there before when we visited their grandparents in California. As we prepared for another trip down there, the older children told the little ones about their first visit to the ocean.

They talked about picking up shells, wading in the waves, and feeling the sand between their toes. They had the little ones so excited that's all they could talk about.

We had a pleasant visit with their grandparents, but all the smaller children could think about was getting to the ocean. My son, Scott, was especially excited. He kept asking, "So, when are we going to the beach?"

The day finally arrived. As we drove through the city traffic, my oldest daughter got them more excited.

"And there's water as far as you can see. And when the sun sets, it's like a whole trail of diamonds."

The younger children started pestering me. "Are we almost there yet?" Scott was especially vocal.

To distract them, I told them to keep a watch and try to be the first to see it. Finally, we went through a short tunnel, and there was the ocean. It wasn't a very big beach, probably no more than fifty yards long, but it was a beach, nonetheless. The younger children started clamoring for me to stop as if we would never see another one.

"Daddy," Scott said, "it's the beach. We need to stop."

I answered him teasingly. "That's so small it's just a son of a beach. Perhaps we should go to a big one."

My wife, Donna, smacked my shoulder. "You shouldn't say those things to the kids. You never know what they'll say."

I had in mind to go to a bigger beach, but the excitement in our rented motorhome grew to the point I had to stop. The older children ran for the beach while Donna and I gathered up the smallest children, along with a myriad of beach towels, diaper bags, and other things we would need. We then hurried after them.

The children played there for hours. We never did go to a bigger beach. They were content just to be on the ocean. We watched the sun set, then finally went back to the motorhome. We went to beaches many more times on our vacation, but the little children relished that first visit the most.

After we got home from our vacation, we went to church. An older gentleman asked Scott what his favorite part of the vacation was.

Scott got excited as he answered. "My favorite part was visiting the son of a beach."

The man's eyes grew wide with shock. And as I tried to explain, Donna smacked my shoulder again. "I told you that you shouldn't say things like that to the children."

The Dress

Terri received a call from her sister, Lori, one morning. They often talked on the phone, but she could tell this call had a special purpose.

"Terri," Lori said, "I need your help in getting rid of a dress."

Terri thought that sounded like a strange request, and she listened as Lori told her the story.

Lori and Terri were both good seamstresses, having learned it from their mother. One day, as a birthday present, Lori was invited by her mother to go with her to pick out some fabric to make a dress. They had spent much of the day together looking at different pieces at the store. Lori finally settled on one that was a bright yellow with lots of flowers on it. It reminded her of sunshine and spring, two of her favorite things. After her mother paid for the cloth, she took Lori to a restaurant, and they had dinner. It was an unforgettable day.

Lori wasted no time making the dress. She had recently had a baby, and she wanted the new dress for when she got the weight off that had come with carrying a child. So, she made it for the size she wore before she got pregnant.

It didn't take her long to make the dress, but getting the weight off was another matter. She kept the dress hanging where she could see it every day as motivation. But try as she might, some of the extra pounds stubbornly refused to leave. The dress became a painful reminder that she would never be her young, trim self again. Lori finally made the decision that it had to go.

She took the dress to a local thrift store. But knowing how much her mother looked forward to seeing her wear it, Lori set out to find the same material. She checked every place within a hundred miles that she knew sold fabric, but there was nothing even close to the same. She also checked online with no luck. She kept a small piece of it in her purse for comparison and checked everywhere she went.

Then on her next birthday, she got a surprise. As a present, her mother presented her with a dress that looked exactly like the one Lori had made. In fact, as Lori looked at it more, she realized it actually was the one she had made.

"I found this at a local thrift shop," her mom proudly said. "It reminded me of the cloth you liked, and I knew you would enjoy it."

Lori thanked her mother and put the dress away. It obviously still didn't fit and continued to remind her of that fact. She finally decided she had to get rid of it again. She didn't want to just throw away such a lovely dress. So, she waited until she thought her mother would have forgotten about it, and when she was in Salt Lake City, four hours from home, she dropped it off at a thrift shop.

That's why it was almost a horrific experience a few weeks later when they had a family dinner and her mother presented her with the same dress. Lori thought that was impossible, but when she checked it over, she found the few tiny flaws that she had made.

Her mother happily shared the story of her purchase. "Your father and I were traveling down to see your brother in Nevada, and I realized I had forgotten my swimsuit. We stopped at a thrift shop in Salt Lake City to get one, and I found this dress. Now you will have many matching dresses."

That was the reason Lori called Terri. "I don't know what to do," Lori said. "It's almost like the dress is possessed and keeps coming back to haunt me to remind me I am bigger than I want to be. I mean, what is the chance Mom could have gone to the same thrift shop where I dropped the dress off? There must be hundreds, if not thousands, of thrift shops in Salt Lake City."

Lori gave the dress to Terri, and Terri promised she

would do something good with it but make it so it would no longer come back to remind Lori of the weight she couldn't lose. Terri used the fabric from the dress in a quilt, feeling that would take care of it.

But one day, their mother saw it. She laughed. "You know what? Lori loves that fabric and even has dresses from it. After she bought some of that material, I went back and bought the last of it from the store. It has been in my sewing room for years as I wondered what to do with it. But you have given me the perfect idea."

"What's that?" Terri asked.

"Since Lori loves it so much, I'm going to make her a whole quilt out of it."

Understanding Passing

The last couple of weeks have been challenging for me. I lost my mother. She was ninety-six. I had watched her health decline and felt I was prepared for the inevitable, but when it came, I wasn't as prepared as I thought.

Mom has been in an assisted living center for the last year and a half. My wife, Donna, and I live close by, so we have been the ones to take her to doctor appointments, to the library, and many other places. As we could see that her time here was coming to an end, we thought we should inform my siblings. But Mom didn't want to feel weak and told me I couldn't. I respected her request but still tried to drop hints to them to help them prepare.

One day, Donna suggested we have a zoom meeting and invite all of Mom's descendants. That is eight living children plus spouses, fifty-six grandchildren, and more than ninety great-grandchildren. Mom liked the idea. We set it for a Sunday evening, and I informed everyone.

But Sunday morning, Mom suddenly started having real problems. Donna and I each received a phone call and rushed there from our different meetings. Mom wasn't doing well, and I didn't think the zoom call was going to happen. But when I started talking about it, things changed. I don't know if it was adrenaline or what the nurse called a final rally, but she perked up and soon asked if I was going to get it on her tv for her.

"Mom," I said, "it's still hours away."

"But don't you need to test it or something?" she asked.

To alleviate her concerns, I connected her tv, and we stared at the picture of our connection for the next two hours. Then people started to connect. There were only a few at first, but soon there were dozens. Mom was so animated I could hardly believe it. She hadn't shown that much energy in months. The call went a long time, far longer than I thought she would have energy for.

When she finished, she was exhausted. She wanted us to eat dinner with her, and we did. By the time dinner was over, she hardly had the strength to sit in her wheelchair. When an aide was helping her into bed, Mom said she didn't think she would be getting up again; and she didn't.

The next morning, she was unresponsive. She didn't want to be alone as she left this life, so we both stayed much of the day. My daughter and I stayed all night while Donna went home to take care of our grandchildren. Donna joined us the next morning, and it wasn't long before Mom left us to join my dad and brothers who had gone before.

I felt like I was in a daze for a couple of days. My siblings came and helped take care of things that needed to be done. I finally started to feel like my mind was clearing and was even able to share humorous stories of Mom at the funeral as she had requested. But what touched me most was listening to the young children trying to understand what was happening and expressing their love and thoughts.

One small niece asked her older sister, "Where is Grandma? Momma said we were coming to see her."

"Grandma has gone to live with Grandpa," the older sister replied.

"Why didn't he just come here and live with Grandma?" the first child asked.

"Because God wanted them both to live with him," the older girl said.

"When is he going to give them back?" the younger girl asked.

"Not for a long time," the older girl answered.

"I don't think that is very nice," the younger girl said. "I think he should give them back now."

When we got to the cemetery, one small boy asked who all the flowers were for. His older sister said, "They are for Grandma."

"But she is gone," the little boy said. "How will she get them?"

The older girl pointed at the sky. "After everyone leaves, angels will come and take them to her in heaven so she will know we love her."

I smiled. Sometimes children say it better than anyone else.

Fathers and Consequences

There was a community breakfast for fathers and their young children. I always enjoyed these. It was not only the good food, but it was fun to share time with my children and their friends. I also enjoyed visiting with the other fathers.

As we waited in line for some pancakes, I saw Jim walk in. Jim was one of my former scouts, but I hadn't seen him in years. Beside him was a miniature model of himself.

I smiled as I shook Jim's hand. "So, this is your little son?"

Jim nodded. "His name is Colter."

Colter was about three years old. I spoke to him and held out my hand. He looked at his dad, and Jim nodded. Colter then shook my hand.

Adam, another of my former scouts, came up with his little daughter. "Hey, Jim," he said, "did you hear about Kevin?"

Jim nodded. I could tell by the expression on Jim's face that he struggled to think about it. Jim and Kevin both came from influential, wealthy families. They had been best friends growing up. In my scout troop, they were inseparable. They always shared the same tent, and where one went, the other went. And when one got in trouble, the other was right there, too.

"You two seemed to have grown apart and gone separate ways," I said. "What happened?"

Jim seemed to want to visit with me alone, so he said nothing until Adam had gone to join some other fathers. Then, as Jim and Colter made their way to the same table as my children and me, he shared his feelings.

"Really, the end of our time together began the night we were arrested," Jim said. "We had done illegal things before but never got caught. We kept doing worse and worse things until the day we were arrested and locked up. I can still remember that night vividly."

Jim told me they were both scared as they sat in the jail cell together. Kevin called his father, and soon his father came and bailed him out of jail. But for Jim, it was different. When he reached his father, his father asked to speak to the police officer. They talked for a while, then the police officer hung up.

"Is my dad coming to get me?" Jim asked.

The policeman shook his head. "Your father said that you need to face the consequences of your actions. You will stay here at least overnight. He just asked that we keep you safe."

Jim's anger at his father burned as he watched Kevin leave. How could his father be so mean as to just leave him there? It was a long night, and by the time his father came the next day, Jim was in no mood to talk to him. That didn't matter, because his father had some things to say.

"Jim," his dad said, "every decision in life carries consequences. Good decisions carry good consequences, but the consequences of bad decisions are usually unpleasant. If you decide to do something you shouldn't, I expect you to honestly pay the price for that decision."

In the court hearing, Kevin's dad hired the best lawyer, and Kevin got off with little mention of what happened. On the other hand, by his father's request, Jim got hours of community service with the offense to be removed from his record upon completion.

"Those service hours made it so I didn't have time to spend with Kevin doing things I shouldn't," Jim said. "They also made me think. I realized it was stupid to do things that got a person jail time or took away their freedom. Kevin kept getting into trouble, and his dad kept bailing him out. He never faced the consequences of what he did. At least, he didn't until this time. He is going to prison for a long time, and even his father can't save him from that."

Jim appeared thoughtful as he continued. "I, on the other hand, have a wonderful wife, a sweet little son, and I feel I have a bright future."

He then summed up his thoughts about what he had shared. "I'm grateful for a father that helped me understand that there are consequences for my actions. I hope I can be just like him with my son."

The Couch

    James taught religion in a small building across the street from a university. The students often saw it as a place where they could not only take a religion class, but could unwind from the stress of college life. There were ping-pong tables and other activities for them to enjoy. But there was one student who used it for another purpose. Stephen would struggle to stay awake in class, and the minute it was over, he was fast asleep on the couch.

    James was concerned that something was wrong. While the other students were busy playing ping-pong, chess, or a multitude of games, the building sounded like the crowd at a rock concert. But the noise didn't seem to bother Stephen at all. He could have slept through a hurricane taking the building away. In fact, taking the building away was kind of what happened one day.

    Once classes were over each day, James would retire to his office to catch up on paperwork. He always left his door open. He enjoyed watching the student activity and wanted to stay available in case a student wanted to visit.

    But on that day, while he was sitting in his office working, he realized that the boisterous noise level had dropped quite a few decibels. He wondered what was going on. He was about to check when the end of the couch appeared in front of his door.

    James watched as the couch moved ever so slowly until the center came into view. It kept moving, and finally the other end appeared. A group of boys were carefully pushing the couch down the hall at a near snail's pace. And, of course, on the couch was Stephen, still sound asleep.

As the boys continued past the door, a smiling, silent crowd behind them was there to egg them on. They just kept streaming slowly past the door. Soon, James knew enough had passed so that the hall past his office must be full. He then heard the click of the outside door opening.

James walked to his office window, and soon he could see the whole procession continuing across the parking lot to a nice grassy area surrounding a volleyball sandlot. At the edge of the grass was a steep curb. The boys surrounded the couch, carefully picked it up, and carried it over to place it in a shady area under some trees.

After they had carefully set the couch down, the group returned to the building. Once inside, there was an almost instant burst of laughter and chatter. The group went back to their games, and James returned to his work but kept glancing out the window at the couch. Stephen slept a long time but finally stirred. He looked around and at first seemed confused, but then he just smiled.

The next day, James invited Stephen into his office to discuss his sleep issues.

"I'm sorry about sleeping in the seminary," Stephen said. "I go to school all day and work much of the night. I seldom get more than a few hours of sleep."

But then Stephen had a question for James. "Sir, do you believe in angels? I mean, you're a religious person and all. But do you?"

"Why do you ask?" James replied.

"Well, I often struggle to get into a deep sleep,"

Stephen said. "But the other day, I dreamed angels were carrying me along on a cloud, and then at the end of the journey, they lifted the cloud up and floated me into paradise. It was the best sleep I have gotten in months. And when I woke up, I was in the shade of trees with a cool breeze floating over me."

Stephen stopped and looked up quizzically. "It was so peaceful and felt like it really happened."

James smiled. "I do believe in angels. But sometimes I think they come in blue jeans and sneakers and aren't even trying to be of service. One just never knows."

Freedom and Peace

Olena sat in my class, staring straight ahead. Her eyes seemed glazed. When I called on her, she didn't respond. I didn't want to embarrass her, so I called on someone else, but I continued to watch her. I could tell that something was dreadfully wrong.

After class was over, Olena moved slowly, as if she was in a daze. I waited until most of the class had left before approaching her.

"Olena, is something wrong?"

She shook her head, but the tears that started coming told a different story. Finally, she dropped into her chair, put her face in her hands, and sobbed. After she had cried for some time, she wiped away her tears.

"Professor Howard," she said, "I don't even know how to explain what I'm feeling right now. There are so many thoughts going through my mind."

She seemed to want to visit, even if it was hard. Eventually, she opened up and talked about it.

"As you know, I am Ukrainian," she said. "I had just come over here to school when Russia invaded our country. My father went to fight while my mother took the rest of the children and fled the country. Since then, I have had no word whether my father is still alive.

"I just got an email from a neighbor telling me that two of my good friends have been killed, and a third one is missing. I'm not sure whether my mother and younger siblings made it out of the country. I don't know where they are."

Olena began to cry again. Eventually, she wiped her eyes once more and told me more.

"My grandfather is almost eighty years old. He lived during much of the Soviet occupation of our country. He talked a lot about the fear and the people that would disappear if they spoke up. He said he would prefer to die than to live that way again, and even at his age, he has gone to fight, too.

"In contrast, this week all my roommates are talking about the Fourth-of-July celebration. They are going to flag-raisings, readings of important documents, barbecues, and lots of firework shows. They have invited me along, but I am struggling in my heart to feel much like celebrating."

She paused briefly and then said some things that I thought were even more profound.

"I have watched in this country and wondered if it could someday face an enemy that might destroy it. The military here is strong, but I wonder if the enemy might come from within. I have watched people try to limit the vote of those who oppose them. I have seen lots of hatred and anger. The only thing that enables Ukraine, a small country compared to Russia, to stand against them, is the unity we have had in joining together to fight.

"I've wondered if a country as powerful as the United States were to let division and differences get in the way, could it open a door for an enemy to gain power? I wonder if that enemy will be one right here, citizens who may try to overthrow the government to take power or retain power."

We talked for quite a while. As she shared her feelings, she seemed to gain more courage to face the unknown ahead of her. But it was her parting words that made me think the deepest about our own freedoms.

"If I have learned anything from watching my own country and then living here," she said, "it is that no one can take peace and freedom for granted. If those are lost, it is hard to get them back."

A Fun Dog

Buster was part of a litter of pups born at our house. We told the children they could have only one dog. They chose Buster, and we gave the other puppies and the mother away to good homes.

I've shared stories about Buster before. He wanted to join the family of a cat with new kittens, but the mother cat would have none of it and drove him away. But one wintry night, when the mother cat couldn't keep her kittens warm, the kittens found their way to Buster and snuggled inside his deep furry coat. The mother cat then adopted Buster as part of her family. It was funny to see her licking him clean, along with all the kittens. When Buster didn't like it and tried to pull away, the mother cat would slap him with her paw. He would then allow her to lick him, even though he was about five times her size.

I shared many other things, but one I haven't was how much he loved our children. We have a big pond, and the children loved swimming in it. When the children walked out of the house in swimsuits, carrying towels, Buster beat them to the yard gate. He knew what that kind of dress meant, and he loved to go swimming.

He also loved balls. The children would take big blow-up beach balls out to the pond with them. They hit them back and forth, often playing keep-away from the child in the center. But often, Buster became the child in the center. The water was only about three feet deep, and the children could stand and hit the ball back and forth. But Buster couldn't stand and have his head above water. He had to swim constantly, and swim he did.

He could swim for hours, back and forth, trying to get the ball. I thought he would grow weary, and sometimes he showed some fatigue, but whenever we decided it was time to get out of the pond, he slowly moped his way back to the yard.

The children worked hard at keep-away from Buster because his only way of catching the ball was with his teeth. We lost about one ball to teeth puncture holes every time we went swimming. But they were cheap, dollar-store balls, so we bought plenty of them.

There was one other thing that Buster got excited about. In our front yard, we often played what the kids called "Daddy Kickball." It was me against all of them. I would pitch, they would kick the ball, and I would use the ball to get them out. These were also lighter balls, so when I threw them at the children to get them out, they didn't hurt. They also didn't go too far, no matter how hard the children kicked them. We could play that game for hours.

Often the children would run all over the yard, trying to avoid getting out, missing the bases altogether. Sometimes, I would get them out because they would eventually collapse into a fit of laughter on the lawn. Even when I got them out, they got to continue around the bases until they got to home plate.

As we played, Buster would run back and forth along the fence that divided the front yard from the back. My children would often ask, "Daddy, can't we let him out?" But I was afraid he would get his teeth in the ball and end the game.

But one day, I gave into their pleadings. Buster was excited to join us. For some reason, the ball didn't become the focus of his attention. Instead, he seemed to think he was supposed to race the children around the bases. Often, this meant he got in the road, and they, or I, tripped over him. It didn't matter to him. He was immediately back up and chasing them to the next base.

But as Buster got older, there was one thing he liked even more than racing the children. Two of our bases were trees growing in the yard, but we had to drag something over for third base. One night, as we were trying to find something for third base, one of the older children called Buster over. She had him lie down at third, and she rubbed his belly. He soon realized that if he stayed there, every time the children came to third, he got a belly rub. From then on, when we played kickball, Buster would bark until we let him out. Then he would go over and lie down at third base, ready for his round of belly rubs.

Buster is gone now, and I miss him. He was the best third base we ever had.

Hamsters and Rabbits

David was away from home and looked forward to the letters from his dad. There were usually interesting family tidbits, with a little bit of dad wisdom. As he started to read the latest one, he smiled.

"As you know, we got three rabbits for Easter. The guy who gave them to us said there were two females and a male. We decided we should get rid of the male before the same thing happened that happened with the hamsters."

David smiled at the thought of the hamsters. He and his brother had each gotten one from a lady who needed to get rid of them. David's hamster was a female, and his brother's was a male.

David's mother was not too excited about the new gifts. She felt hamsters were nothing more than fluffy mice. But David thought they were cute. In fact, he considered that it would be fun to have a whole bunch of them. The dollar signs whirred in his mind as he considered selling them and making a fortune, forgetting he got his for free because the person couldn't get rid of them.

He read all about hamsters. If he worked it out right, he could own around seven baby hamsters in around twenty-one days. He sneaked his hamster in with his brother's a few times, and sure enough, less than a month later, there were baby hamsters in the bottom of the cage.

David's mother was not happy. It wasn't hard for her to figure out what had happened. And, as the hamsters got bigger, it was almost impossible to keep the males and females separated. Soon, there were so many hamsters that David's mother claimed their house was being overrun with "hairy mice" that they couldn't give away.

David went back to reading his dad's letter.

"We decided we should give away the male rabbit, so I called Walt about it. Do you remember him? He is the guy that lives just down the road and raises lots of rabbits. He was happy to take the male.

"We took the rabbit down there and thought all was well. But about a month later, one of the females had babies. I couldn't believe it. I thought we had gotten rid of the male in time. But I figured she must have gotten pregnant just before we gave him away. But then, a few months later, she had babies again. Apparently, our other rabbit we named Jill was really Jack. So that meant the one we gave away was a female.

"We decided to trade the one we now knew was a male for her. Walt was good to make the switch, and we thought our problems were over. But then, about a month later, the female we got back had babies. Either she was bred while at Walt's house, or there is a wild, rogue male rabbit sneaking into pens at night.

"We have tried to separate the males from the females, but after this episode of events, I am beginning to doubt my ability to distinguish the difference. Anyway, we have more rabbits than we know what to do with. If you could use one, let us know.

"I wonder if the postal service can ship rabbits parcel post. I could send one to everyone I know."

First Calculator

I had just worked an algebra problem on the chalkboard and told my students to do the calculation on their calculator. Before they could punch it in, I told them what I thought it should be. This is a good way for them to check and see if they punched it in correctly. One student expressed her amazement.

"How can you calculate so fast, and without a calculator?"

I laughed. "I grew up before the days of calculators. We had to calculate everything we did by hand. So those of us who had lots of math or science classes often got so we could calculate things in our head."

"Wow!" one boy said. "You must be older than you look. I can't even imagine not having a calculator."

"What was the first calculator you used?" another boy asked.

"Well," I replied, "if I remember right, the calculator was a Hewlett-Packard one. Other companies were already starting to produce calculating machines, but some were too big to carry around. The story I heard was that one of the two owners of Hewlett-Packard got tired of doing engineering calculations by hand. He told his engineers to make a machine that could do the basic four functions, add, subtract, multiply, and divide, and would fit in his pocket.

"The engineering team got busy with the new assignment. After a year, the appointed time to have the machine ready, they had something that was fairly good, but bigger than desired. I heard that when their boss was out of town, they went to his wife and got all his shirts and had them tailored with bigger pockets. If they couldn't make the calculator fit the pocket, they would make the pocket fit the calculator."

The students laughed at that. Then a girl raised her hand. "Today, calculators have lots more than just those four simple functions. There are logs, square roots, and all sorts of things. How did you do those without a calculator?"

"That is a good question," I replied. "In those days, we had a shelf in the math and science rooms with books of tables. The tables for logs, for example, would have a list of log values in increments of one-tenth. If the number you needed wasn't there, you used interpolation, a method of using the other numbers, to approximate the value you needed. There were similar tables for sines, cosines, tangents, and roots. It could be quite tedious."

"What was it like getting your first calculator?" a boy asked.

"I was in college when I got my first calculator," I replied. "But the first one I used was in high school. I was a junior in a chemistry class. We had been working on learning how to use the slide rule to do calculations. Then a school board member told us they had purchased three calculators for the classroom, one for each table. The calculators cost $250 each, but we could forgo spending half the semester mastering the slide rule."

"Wow!" a girl said. "That is a lot to pay for a calculator."

I nodded. "And that was with a discount. It mostly only did the four functions, but it tried to approximate logs and things using built-in tables. But its logs, roots, and trig functions often weren't accurate enough for what we did.

"Another thing about them was they had to be plugged in. So, an electric box was wired at the center of each table. We had to pass the calculator up and down the table during tests. We were always told to clear it before passing it. And sometimes the calculator would overheat and shut off, usually in the middle of a test because of heavy usage."

"Sounds like my brain," a girl said. Everyone laughed.

"So, what was the changeover like to using calculators in a math class?" a boy asked.

"I'll tell you what," I replied. "I'll share some of that another day. Right now, we need to finish the lesson so you will be prepared to do your homework."

The students nodded, but one student said she could hardly wait to hear more.

(Continued)

Calculators and a Changing World

My students were fascinated to learn that I had never used a calculator until just before going to college. I promised them I would tell them about what the change was like before class started the next time. Most of the students were in class early, eager to hear.

"It may seem really strange," I said, "but one of the biggest challenges came with determining which classes should have calculators and which should not."

"Didn't they just allow them in all classes once they were available?" a boy asked.

"Not at all," I replied. "In most of my college classes, calculators were banned. The teachers felt that a calculator was a crutch and made it so the student didn't have to think. I had teachers who, besides paper and a pencil, only allowed an abacus and a slide rule. I was not efficient at either and usually got faster answers using just the pencil, paper, and approximations.

"The debate about whether calculators should be allowed raged in math circles and math conferences I attended for over a decade after I first used one. Some felt calculators should be banned entirely from the campus environment. At the other end of the spectrum were those who felt the calculator would take away the drudgery of calculating, making it possible to teach more profound and more important subject matter.

"I must admit that I was somewhere in between. I often felt the energy spent on calculation was a useless waste of time, but was required so a student could show they could follow a problem through to the end. On the other hand, having learned how to do math mentally, I felt that there was a certain amount of deep thinking that went into those calculations.

"As time went on, many of us, myself included, felt that the problem wasn't the calculator but the need to change our method of teaching. I had experienced this in my computer classes. Some schools wanted to stay with older, dying languages, such as Fortran and Pascal, while most of the world was changing to more modern programming languages like C and C++. I could see that it was good for students to understand Fortran, but they needed to be prepared in C and C++. But some teachers didn't want to make that change just because they felt it was too much work.

"One spring, I went to a big math conference. The main event was a roundtable discussion on the calculator issue by some of the greatest experts of math education. They were split equally on both sides of the issue. It ended up being more like a debate with a few heated exchanges, some from audience members with those on the stage. At the end of the discussion, a man rose and asked if he could read a quote. The moderator gave permission, and the man started to read.

"I can't remember it exactly, but the educator in the quote said that if we allowed everyone access to this new technology, the nonthinker would appear to be brilliant, while those who thought deeply might appear as fools. Everyone could appear intelligent, whether they had anything of intellectual value to share or not. Therefore, he said the invention should be banned.

"As he finished reading the quote, some of those who favored banning calculators clapped. When they finished, the person reading the quote announced that the person who had given the quote was an educator from the 1600's and was referencing the invention of the pencil."

At this point, my students laughed. A girl asked, "Did they really have a similar debate over the invention of the pencil?"

I nodded. "Apparently so. They felt that making it possible for anyone to write, not just those who had lots of money, would open the gates to many idiotic ideas. But that discussion was the beginning of the end of the fight against students having calculators.

"Today, we have changed how we teach, spending more time helping students learn concepts and less time struggling through the calculations."

A student nodded and said, "How grateful I am that you do."

Ring Tones

I was sitting in a meeting recently when a person's phone went off. His ring tone is a quacking duck. He is getting older and his phone is usually turned way up, so all discussion stopped. The person who owned the phone pretended he was looking around the room to see who the culprit was, even as he tried to nonchalantly shut it off.

He was not fooling anyone, and I'm sure he knew it. Everyone in the meeting had heard that quack quack before, and they all smiled. But it did lead to a fun discussion about ring tones after the meeting. I've heard some funny stories about them I thought I'd share.

One lady said that when her mother passed away, her sister had a singing ring tone. It sang, "What Doesn't Kill You Makes You stronger." It just happened to go off when the family was in the funeral home looking at caskets.

Another lady said they lived on a really busy road. Without her knowledge, her teen son changed her ring tone to a motorcycle revving. All day long she was checking to see who the rude person was that was making so much noise. She could never catch the culprit. When she mentioned it later that evening, her son got a good laugh out of it. And to top things off, she realized she had missed a lot of calls during the day.

A third lady said her phone was always set to the good old-fashioned ring that phones made when everyone had landlines. She had a habit of always waiting until the second ring to pick it up. This lady owned a gold macaw parrot that was thirty years old. The bird had heard the ring a lot and knew the routine. When he heard it, whether on a phone, tv, or anywhere else, he waited until after the second ring and then said, "Hello."

Another lady said her son had changed his father's ring tone to say, "WARNING! It's the wife," whenever she called. She was okay with it, but her husband was not.

My favorite ring tone story was one a man told. He had to get a new phone because his went defunct. Trying to save money, he had gotten a used one that was still in decent shape. It was sold by someone who wanted to upgrade to the newest and greatest model.

He got the phone and took it to the cell phone store to activate it. The young lady that helped him said it would be some time before the phone was live. She did promise him it would work within twenty-four hours.

"Will it signal me when it starts working?" the man asked.

The helper shook her head. "Once it does, it will just work the next time you try to make a call, or if someone calls you."

The man heard someone whistling in his house in the middle of the night. His wife was asleep beside him, and no one else was living there. He sat up, considering that someone must have broken into their home.

He grabbed a gun to defend himself, then cautiously made his way to the sound. What confused him was why the person would whistle, then stop, then whistle again. In fact, why would an intruder whistle at all? And to add to the mystery, the person kept whistling the same phrase over and over. Were they trying to draw him to them? Was he walking into a trap?

Trembling, with his gun raised in front of him, he came around the corner into the room where the intruder was. That was when he saw the light on his phone, and it dawned on him what was happening.

"In my anxious state," he said, "I could have killed my cell phone and had to buy another one. And all of that for someone trying to get me to renew my car warranty."

If you enjoyed this book, please leave a review on Amazon at:

https://www.amazon.com/dp/1629860271

Would you like to see the Life's Outtakes column running in your local paper or magazine? Suggest it to the editor. If an editor runs the Life's Outtakes column due to your suggestion, we will send you a free autographed book by Daris Howard. Find out more here:

http://www.darishoward.com

Read stories, purchase books, or subscribe to our short story list by going to

http://www.publishinginspiration.com

Daris Howard's Amazon page:

http://amzn.com/e/B004H76UGK

For inspiring plays and books, as well as discounts for booksellers, go to

http://www.publishinginspiration.com

About the Author

Daris Howard, an award-winning author and playwright, grew up on an Idaho farm. He was a state champion athlete, competed in college athletics, and lived for a time in New York.

Daris has worked as a cowboy, as a mechanic, in farming, and in the timber industry. He is now a college professor. He has also been a scoutmaster, having up to eighteen boys in his scout troop at a time. In his wide range of experience, he has associated with many colorful characters who form a basis for his writing. Daris has had plays translated into German and French, and his plays have been performed in many countries around the world. For many years, Daris has written the popular column Life's Outtakes, which consists of weekly short stories and is published in various newspapers and magazines in the US and Canada.